SUMMER
OF THE
Zeppelin

ELSIE McCUTCHEON

PUFFIN BOOKS

Puffin Books, Penguin Books Ltd, Harmondsworth, Middlesex, England
Penguin Books, 40 West 23rd Street, New York, New York 10010, U.S.A.
Penguin Books Australia Ltd, Ringwood, Victoria, Australia
Penguin Books Canada Ltd, 2801 John Street, Markham, Ontario, Canada L3R 1B4
Penguin Books (N.Z.) Ltd, 182–190 Wairau Road, Auckland 10, New Zealand

First published by J. M. Dent & Sons Ltd 1983
Published in Puffin Books 1984

Printed and bound in Great Britain by
Cox & Wyman Ltd, Reading
Set in Bembo

Contents

For Norman Roberts,
my nephew and godson

1

Grey Ghosts and Goosegrass

Despite the open windows the temperature in the classroom had soared that afternoon, flushing faces, making scalps prickle and palms too moist to hold pens. Even Mr Christmas, headmaster of Frissington St Peter school, was twitching and perspiring, pulling occasionally at his collar, as he gave Standards 5 and 6 their customary afternoon 'chat'. His voice droned and buzzed around Elvira's dozy brain like some persistent honeybee, making her eyes so heavy-lidded that she was forced to jerk them abruptly away from their contemplation of Lizzie Pitt's blonde sausage-ringlets and stare through the window at the vivid greens of the May countryside and the uncompromising blue of the sky.

In Mr Spurgeon's cornfield on the other side of School Lane, Elvira could see two men manoeuvring the horse-hoe across clay that was baked and crazily cracked from the drought. Before the War it had been her father's job to lead old Toby, the chestnut Suffolk Punch who pulled the hoe, while another man gripped the steerage-handles at the back to keep the gleaming metal shares running in their channels between the rows of springing wheat. Today the work was being done by alien figures in drab, grey uniforms. Germans — prisoners from the Camp at the Old Factory which stood on the hill halfway between Frissington St Peter and Frissington Angel where Elvira lived. And there were prisoners in the next field, too, hand-hoeing thistles out of the corn, working in a long line that kept moving slowly to the left like a thin, grey wave.

It seemed a long time since the German prisoners had been brought to the Old Factory, although in fact it was only eight months. Elvira could remember the October morning vividly because, for a few moments of it, she had been more scared than she had ever been in her life. She had been running down Factory Hill so as not to be late for school, her boots skidding and stumbling over the loose flints of the rough road. There had been a mist lying over the fields and in the valley, and skeletal fingers of it had crept uphill to hover over the hedges and brimming ditches. Elvira had been about fifty yards from the factory gates when the figures had suddenly appeared, a double column of them — grey, ghostly workers — or so she thought — trooping silently through the wide, brick-pillared gateway into a factory that had been closed for the past thirty years. Elvira's legs had weakened and she had sat down hard on the wet grass of the bank, the pounding of her heart shutting out every other sound. Then through the mists had burst a figure in a uniform she couldn't fail to recognize: a British army sergeant! And one who was gesticulating in an extremely lively and unghostlike fashion. The drumming in Elvira's ears had faded and the soldier's rasping voice had torn through the haze to dispel the last remnants of her terror.

"HALT! You German *dummkopfs*!" she had heard him yell a moment later behind the high factory wall. "We've arrived! This is it! Home, sweet home until the end of the War. Understand? . . . *Verstehen*?"

With a sigh of relief Elvira had picked up her dinner-bag and continued on her way. Yet by the time she reached the first of the cottages that straggled down both sides of the hill to Frissington St Peter crossroads, she was already having misgivings. Germans were better than ghosts, certainly. But how much better? She remembered the tales she had heard of how they had murdered Belgian babies and children. And Mr Christmas had brought in a postcard one day showing a group of monstrous-looking German soldiers, with red bloated faces and glassy green eyes, waving swords and wearing spiked helmets. Certainly, the last time Elvira's dad had been home on leave, he had said this was all nonsense, that German soldiers were much the same as British ones and hated the fighting and the trenches every bit as much. Elvira had not been convinced, though. On the morning that the Germans had arrived in Frissington, a lot of locals had shared Elvira's apprehension. They had gathered outside Mrs Fisher's grocery which was on the right-hand side of Factory Hill just before the crossroads.

2

And as Elvira had passed, Mrs Fisher, her sleeves rolled up and her fat, red arms folded across her white pinafore, was declaiming that it was a scandal and a disgrace and that the local people ought to have been consulted before such a decision was taken.

"We don't want the monsters here!" she had shouted, black eyes snapping. "We were told it was our own wounded soldiers they were bringing to the Old Factory . . . Everyone knows the only good Hun is a dead one!" she had finished, to a burst of patriotic cheering. The Germans had stayed, though, despite Mrs Fisher and the petitions she kept organizing to send to important people. Elvira watched the pair who were plodding patiently up and down with the horse-hoe and realized with a little jolt of amazement that they were in fact now part of the Frissington landscape. One expected to see them out in the fields, ploughing or harrowing or singling sugar beet. To begin with she had been afraid to pass the Old Factory, knowing that the Germans were in there. But she had soon become accustomed to seeing them in groups of ten or twelve being marched to work out on the farms. She still hated confronting them, and would cut through the fields if she saw them marching along the road towards her.

Only once had she come directly up against any. That had been on one darkening January afternoon when she had been late in collecting her little brother, Arthur, from Mrs Boniface who looked after him. She had run the pram out of Mrs Boniface's gate and almost collided with a German prisoner, one of a group that had just marched across Frissington Angel green on the way back to the Camp. Elvira's heart had given a terrible lurch when the German had suddenly bent over the pram, for she had thought he was going to harm little Arthur. The toddler had given a chuckle of delight though, and when the man moved away Elvira saw that Arthur was holding a small green and gold motor car in his hand. She had taken it from him and had found to her amazement that it had been very cleverly made out of a syrup tin. As she stood there inspecting the toy in the wintry dusk, with the sound of the

3

Germans' tramping feet fading into the distance, a shudder of apprehension had passed over her. Despite Arthur's outraged yells Elvira had shoved the car into her coat pocket, determined that Rhoda (who was Arthur's mother and Elvira's stepmother) should give her approval before the toy was returned to the little boy. And for once Rhoda had been full of praise for Elvira's action.

"There could be poison paint on that! Or anything! Anything!" Rhoda had exclaimed fearfully, holding the little car between her thumb and index finger. "I shall take it into our factory tomorrow and throw it in the rubbish pit, Elvie!"

Elvira had nodded in full agreement. After all, hadn't Mr Christmas delivered a lecture the previous day on the possibility of poisoned sweets being dropped from enemy aircraft? She had looked down fondly on her two-and-a-half-year-old brother who, still tearful, was marching his soldiers across the rug. One day he might appreciate the fact that she had rescued him from the cruel talons of the enemy.

"ELVIRA PRESTON!"

The headmaster's stentorian voice and the crash of his fat, red English dictionary plummeting on to her desk combined to produce an explosion that shot Elvira out of her reverie with a startled little squeal. There was a fizz of laughter from the class. Mr Christmas rounded on them, his slightly bowed shoulders quivering with anger, his face mottled above his drooping moustache.

"I do not think this is a laughing matter!" he exclaimed in the staccato voice he adopted when enraged. "For five minutes I have been instructing you in how you may make a contribution . . . a small, but vital contribution . . . to the War Effort. And this girl," (he gripped Elvira by the shoulder and shook her) "Elvira Preston here, has not attended to one single word. If the country were full of Elvira Prestons we would be under the Kaiser's heel tomorrow!" He looked down on Elvira with distaste. "Stand!" he commanded her.

Elvira stood. As on many a previous occasion she quivered with nerves and felt that every trembling fragment of her was

4

pulsating with loathing for Mr Christmas.

"As your classmates have already heard," the headmaster addressed her, snapping off each word, "I have promised the services of this school in the collecting of certain wild plants which are to be used to help the country through its present emergency. Goosegrass is one of them . . . you may know the plant as 'cleavers'. It can be used to make coffee substitute, and for medicinal purposes. Each of you will be paid one farthing for every two pounds of the plant you bring in. I expect you to start collecting today, after school, and to bring in at least one pound of goosegrass tomorrow morning. Understood, Elvira?"

"But, I can't sir! I won't have time!" Elvira's dismay was so profound that she gave voice to it spontaneously. The effect on Mr Christmas was dire. His face flushed a uniform dark red and the veins on his right temple stood out, looking exactly like the River Po and its tributaries on the map of Italy in the school atlas.

"You idle, selfish girl!" he upbraided her, in a voice that shook with emotion. "Don't you realize that we are fighting for our lives? That across the narrow strip of English Channel there are hordes of evil men who would make every Briton a slave?"

"She ought to . . . since her dad's over there fighting them!" a voice commented clearly from the centre of the classroom. It was a rough Cockney voice that seemed out of place in a Suffolk school.

"SILENCE, CLARENCE RAE!" Mr Christmas roared, provoked now into a full-blooded fury. "I will not brook impertinence. Go out and stand by my desk. I'll deal with you when I have dismissed the others."

Elvira's brow knitted with irritation as she watched a tall, skinny boy, whose jacket and trousers were sizes too small for him, shuffle out to stand resignedly before the class. Why did Clarry always have to interfere, she thought? It inevitably ended in his being given two strokes of the cane, and it invariably put Mr Christmas in a worse temper than ever. As though

5

to confirm this, the headmaster gave Elvira a final vicious prod in the back with an index finger that was permanently stained with royal-blue ink.

"And I want at least one pound of goosegrass from you tomorrow morning, my lady! Understand?" he said harshly, waiting until Elvira had reluctantly nodded, before he signalled her to sit down. He then strode to the front to dismiss the class.

Five minutes later, standing just outside the school porch, Elvira heard the whistle and slap of the cane as it descended twice on Clarry Rae's crossed palms. She gazed across at a hedgerow that waded in milky pools of Jack-by-the-hedge and campion whose green recesses were alive with twittering birdsong and felt abysmally unhappy. She could see the line of German prisoners still hoeing in the corn and she hated them. The War was their fault. Everyone said so. And it just went on and on and made everything so miserable! Because of it her dad had been fighting in France for three whole years, leaving Elvira to make the best of things with her stepmother and little Arthur. And it wasn't much of a 'best', Elvira thought bitterly. It was the War too that had taken their headmistress, Miss Allison, off to work in a munitions factory in far-away Gretna, and had brought that beastly Mr Christmas and his obnoxious sneak of a grand-daughter to Frissington St Peter. Elvira missed her headmistress almost as much as she missed her dad.

Finally she heard Clarry dismissed by the headmaster and he started tramping along the corridor towards the door. Elvira looked up into the flawless blue canopy of the sky thinking of an old book of Rhoda's that she had recently started reading. It was called *Ivy* and Elvira had just reached a part in the story where Ivy, the heroine, escaped the workhouse by running off with her little brother to a secret smugglers' cave beside the sea. How blissful, Elvira thought, to be able to run away from Mr Christmas and Rhoda's nagging and all the chores! From little Arthur too who was sometimes the biggest chore of all! But it was a pretty hopeless dream since the sea was over thirty miles away and there wasn't likely to be even a tiny cave hereabouts. With a sigh she turned to greet Clarry whose wide mouth curved into a grin at the sight of her and who came bounding down the three porch steps in a single, ungainly leap.

2

Declaration of War

"You shouldn't interfere, Clarry! It doesn't do any good," Elvira remonstrated with the boy as they started up Factory Hill past Mrs Fisher's shop.

Mrs Fisher was sitting in the open doorway knitting a khaki sock. She fixed them with a marble eye as they passed her, not because they had annoyed her in any way, but because Rhoda was now buying all her rationed goods in Ipswich and Mrs Fisher felt snubbed.

"Can't help it. Old Christmas gets up my nose," Clarry retorted, shuffling along beside Elvira like an unhappy scarecrow. "What was all the fuss about anyway?" he asked after a moment. "Why can't you pick his old grass for him, Elvie?" Exasperation furrowed Elvira's brow again.

"Well, it's obvious, isn't it?" she almost wailed, wiping a bead of perspiration from her nose. "As soon as I get home I've to collect Arthur from Mrs Boniface. Then, as there isn't a drop of drinkable water left in Frissington Angel because of the drought, I've to trail right back to the pump – with a great, heavy bucket in one hand and dragging Arthur with the other!" Elvira glared viciously across at the pump whose handle was being energetically worked by a woman holding a bonneted baby on her left arm.

"Ain't you got water nearer than that, Elvie?" Clarry queried, his thin eyebrows shooting up.

"We've got a pond," Elvira told him. "Dirty, green, slimy old thing. But Rhoda won't have any of that. Not even for washing."

7

She started off again up the hill and Clarry shortened his long strides to match hers.

"Half-after-five it'll be by the time I get that dratted water home," Elvira continued grumblingly. "Then I've to find Arthur something to eat and start the dinner so's it'll be ready when Rhoda gets home from the factory . . . in one of her moods, too, I shouldn't wonder! And after that there's the clearing up, washing Arthur and getting him to bed, and anything else Rhoda can think of," she finished bitterly.

"Least you can get enough to eat when you're doing the cooking," Clarry commented wistfully, and Elvira, glancing down at the boy's stick-like legs and the band of white skin where his frayed trousers and holey socks failed to meet, felt a pang of remorse.

Clarry was one of the 'home' boys, who had been brought to Frissington St Peter in 1915 when the Zeppelins had started bombing London. He had once told Elvira that the proper title of the home where he had been brought up was Parkinson's Institution for Orphaned Boys and that there were always exactly fifteen boys in it. At the moment twelve-year-old Clarry was the oldest there by four years, and he was continually hungry, since the matron, Miss Flint, insisted he must have the same portions as the seven and eight-year-olds. In the winter, especially, things had been bad for him as the Old Rectory, in which the boys had been given accommodation, was wretchedly cold and draughty and Clarry, who had out-grown all his warm winter clothes, was given no new ones to replace them. In the end George Pollitt's mother had given him an old jacket and corduroy trousers, but his boots had been so full of holes that in rainy or snowy weather he had been unable to go to school.

"Isn't old Flintstones any better, then?" Elvira asked Clarry sympathetically. They were slowing down as they approached the iron gates of the Old Rectory on the right-hand side of the road.

"Nup! She just gets worser . . . and worser!" Clarry had a comedian's face with a wide mouth that always seemed on the

8

verge of a grin, and crinkling, humorous eyes. But, all at once, as he attempted to joke, his cheerful mask slipped momentarily to reveal his true unhappiness.

"She's not so bad with the little 'uns," he went on. "But she reckons I'm a real thorn in her flesh. Always wanting something, she says! More food! More clothes! She screeches at me something awful, Elvie! That's a fact!"

Elvira stood outside the gates for a few moments, her brown eyes concerned as she watched Clarry slouch away despondently along the elm-lined driveway. Maybe she wasn't so badly off after all, she reflected. At least she had family. A dad, a half-brother, and Gran and Granfer Preston, though she hadn't seen them since they moved to Yorkshire seven years ago. Perhaps even a stepmother like Rhoda was better than nothing. And maybe she ought to try harder to please her. After all it must have been hard for Rhoda having to leave little Arthur with Mrs Boniface while she went to work in a factory making parts for aeroplanes. She often said she'd only taken the job to help end the War more quickly and bring Elvira's dad back home.

Elvira's new-formed resolution sent her scurrying home instead of dawdling to inspect birds' nests as she normally did. The square windows at the top of the Old Factory squinted down through iron bars now, over the six-foot-high brick wall, giving the building a sinister aspect even in the bright sunlight. Elvira was glad to pass it and jog on uphill past fields of ruffling green barley and wheat, until the dusty, flint-strewn track levelled out and the first of Frissington Angel's ramshackle cottages came into view. After twenty yards or so the road branched right and left to encircle Frissington Angel's wide green on which a couple of donkeys and some geese were grazing. Elvira took the right fork and ran in at the gate of a tidy-looking, brick-built cottage to collect her little brother from Mrs Boniface at the back door. Arthur, who always became inordinately boisterous on Elvira's arrival, insisted on running along to their own cottage with two chubby arms encircling Elvira's waist. Elvira humoured him until she had collected the water bucket from the lean-to scullery at the back, then she gripped him firmly by the right hand and told him to be "Elvie's best boy".

"Will Artie get cake, then?" he asked, his blue eyes considering her calculatingly.

"Maybe," Elvira conceded with a smile.

It was a hot, dusty, wearisome trek back to the Frissington St Peter pump. To begin with, as always, Elvira encouraged Arthur's little legs to trot along by chanting nursery rhymes with him. They started with 'Jack and Jill', Elvira having altered the first line to 'went *down* the hill' to fit the occasion. By the time they passed the Old Rectory gates though, Arthur was starting to drag on Elvira's pinafore and occasionally sitting on the road and refusing to budge until coaxed. The return journey was ten times more wearisome, too, because it was uphill for most of the way and Elvira was carrying the filled bucket from which she was determined not to spill a single drop. This was where Elvira usually had to resort in desperation to 'Little Orphant Annie', a rather scary poem which she had once memorized for the Christmas concert at school. Rhoda had forbidden her ever to recite it to Arthur since he had had a nightmare about it, but Arthur could never have enough of it, especially the verse about the 'little boy who wouldn't say his prayers' who was stolen by the goblins. When Elvira read the final line in her most sepulchral voice . . . "And the goblins'll get *you* if you don't watch out" . . . Arthur would run screeching on ahead and cover ten yards without realizing it.

In the end even 'Little Orphant Annie' began to wear thin. Arthur's face became ever redder and crosser-looking, and the sun beat down relentlessly on Elvira's back, scorching her through the thick cotton of her long-sleeved blouse.

"Oh, rain! Rain! Why ever can't you rain?" she burst out suddenly, glaring up at the serene, blue sky.

Arthur, excited by the chanting of the words, began to hop up and down, making Elvira's bucket joggle alarmingly.

"Rain, rain, rain, rain!" he yelled in his raucous little voice.

10

The Prestons' whitewashed cottage was the last of the houses on the southern side of Frissington Angel green. It had two smallish bedrooms upstairs, a lean-to scullery and a decent-sized living-room downstairs. The front door led directly into the living-room, but was never opened because a large, horsehair sofa had been pulled across it.

It was from under this sofa that Elvira dragged Arthur's small toy box when they finally arrived home. Then, having given him a slice of cake and a cup of milk, she settled him down to play while she attended to the dinner. Rhoda had brought lamp-chops home with her the evening before and put them into the hanging-larder which Elvira's dad had fixed up at the side of the cottage, so that it was always in the shade of the apple tree. Elvira ran out now to open the perforated metal door of the larder and bring the chops in on their covered dish. Using a single match from the box on the mantleshelf, she skilfully lit the fire that was laid in the big, black range. Matches were very scarce nowadays. Everything was scarce, Elvira thought morosely. Usually she stewed their meat, cooking it in the biggest pot along with the potatoes and carrots. But it suddenly occurred to Elvira that she could fry the chops, use the small pot for the vegetables and thus save some of the precious water. The vegetables needed little pre-paration, having been scrubbed clean the night before, and soon Elvira was humming contentedly as she watched the coal glow red behind the iron bars of the range and heard the pot on the top begin to bubble gently. She set three places at the scrubbed deal table, waiting until the vegetables were fairly cooked before pushing the pot to one side and setting the heavy frying-pan in its place. By the time the rickety little gate finally creaked open to admit Rhoda, everything was ready to be dished up.

"How's my baby, then?" Rhoda crooned, lifting little Arthur up lovingly as he hurled himself against her legs in exuberant delight.

A truck from the factory brought Rhoda and her workmates to Frissington St Peter crossroads each evening and Rhoda was still in her working uniform of long blue tunic, trousers and a round little cap. She had rosy cheeks and very bright, dark eyes that now looked across enquiringly at Elvira.

"Any letter from your dad?" she asked anxiously. Rhoda left for work at seven-thirty every morning, an hour before old George the postman started to push his bicycle slowly up Factory Hill. For weeks now Rhoda had asked the same question as soon as she stepped in the door.

"No . . . not yet," Elvira replied for the umpteenth time. Rhoda lowered Arthur to the floor, her face clouding.

"That's four weeks now!" she said tersely. "Four weeks and not a line! There must be something wrong."

"I expect he just hasn't time," Elvira replied matter-of-factly, turning to prod the chops with a long fork. "Mr Christmas says there's furious fighting at Ypres again and that his cousin up in Southwold can hear the guns ever so clear!"

"Elvira! What are you doing there? You haven't *fried* the chops!" Rhoda, eyes sparkling dangerously, crossed over to push Elvira roughly aside.

"I thought it would save water," Elvira explained.

But her stepmother whirled round on her furiously. "You really are a thoughtless little madam!" she raged. "Now we'll have Arthur up with tummy-ache all night eating fried meat at bedtime. I'll swear you do these things on purpose to make life harder, Elvira! I'll swear you do!" She stalked upstairs to take off her working clothes and wash in the half-inch of water Elvira had poured into the bowl in her bedroom.

Elvira continued to prod at the lamb-chops, tears hot as the burning coals in the range, pricking behind her lids. "Elvie bad girl! Elvie bad girl!" Arthur sang softly to himself, as he pushed a wooden engine around the floor. So this was all the thanks she got, Elvira thought bitterly! After all her good resolutions. And all her hard work. She knew she could never mean as much to Rhoda as either her dad or little Arthur did. But sometimes lately she really had begun to think her step-mother hated her. She couldn't do anything right nowadays in Rhoda's eyes. Whatever she said caused offence. Well, maybe

Rhoda was in for a shock, Elvira resolved, suddenly spearing a chop viciously and holding it aloft before dropping it again into the sizzling fat. Maybe this particular worm would turn, and very shortly too! The evening meal would have been eaten in silence, had it not been for Arthur's babyish prattle. And, as soon as Elvira had finished, she stood up.

"I'm off out now," she announced, tightening the ribbon at the nape of her neck that held back her heavy mane of brown hair. "The school's collecting goosegrass for the War Effort."

Rhoda's mouth dropped open. "But what about the clearing-up?" she demanded, when she'd found her voice. "What about the evening chores?"

"You'll just have to do them yourself for once, won't you?" Elvira retorted, standing straight-backed, her eyes, pebbly-hard, locking with Rhoda's, until her stepmother gave a sigh of exasperation and turned away.

3

A Way Through the Trees

Elvira was still inwardly seething as she turned left outside the gate and started back towards Frissington St Peter. She could see the little Coopers, and Cecil and Mary Larter with their baskets on the far side of the green. They were heading in the opposite direction, past the smithy along towards Frissington Angel church which sat back from the road on a little mound so that its grey tower was visible from every part of the village. Elvira remembered now that there was an abundance of goosegrass in the overgrown little churchyard, but she didn't feel like company at that moment, especially not tittering eight and nine-year-olds.

Elvira was the oldest school pupil in Frissington Angel, now that Albert Taylor and Vera Samson had passed their Labour Certificates and left school to start work. Elvira could also have left school had she wanted to. She had had her twelfth birthday in February and she would easily have passed the

Labour Certificate test. Vera said the sums and the spelling were easy and that the reading wasn't too difficult, either. Vera was working in a baker's shop now in Bingham Market and earning six shillings a week. But Elvira's dad wanted her to stay on at school and would have liked her to try for a free place in Bingham Market grammar school. Miss Allison, who was the real headmistress of Frissington St Peter school and who would be coming back when the War ended, had thought that Elvira had a good chance of winning a grammar school place. But after Mr Christmas had come to the school, Elvira's work had rapidly deteriorated until she was in the lower half of the class, and there had been no point in her sitting the scholarship examination.

The thought of Mr Christmas reminded Elvira of the reason for her excursion and she slowed her pace and began to search the banks for the long, angular stems of goosegrass. She finally spied a whole mesh of it on the right-hand bank, just where a wheatfield ended and a small coppice began. Hoisting her skirt up, she crossed the ditch with a single stride and wriggled through the wire fence to stand on the edge of the field. A narrow, grassy path divided the growing crop from the untidy fringe of the coppice, and all along this path goosegrass was rife. Elvira began to make her way up the gently sloping path, picking all the time and dropping the long grasses into her pinafore, to which they attached themselves by the tiny spines on the backs of their sword-shaped leaves. She had never been in this field before because until last autumn it had been a meadow enclosed by thick, prickly hedgerows, where cattle and occasionally a bellowing bull had been put to graze. Now, however, because the country's corn supplies were running low, every inch of ground was precious. Last September the old hedges had been burned down and the field put under winter wheat.

Dad would miss that long stretch of hedgerow by the roadside, Elvira reflected as she wandered on. It had been a proper storehouse of good things: crab-apples, hips and haws, blackberries, and holly, for decorating at Christmastime. When there had been just the two of them they had always come to that hedgerow during Christmas week, and Dad had hoisted Elvira up on his shoulders so that she could reach the best holly branches and cut them off with his sharp little knife. Rhoda had put an end to that by insisting that it was much too dangerous and that Elvira could easily lop a finger off if the razor-sharp knife were to slip. And Dad had listened and finally agreed . . . as he always did with Rhoda. So that after that they had had to be content with the second-best holly. Elvira reached the top end of the field and felt suddenly leg-weary. Ahead of her was another strip of coppice, but a suffi-ciently narrow one to show large patches of pink and gold evening sky through the gaps in the trees. With a sigh she turned to sit down on the grassy headland, gazing back down on the road where a horse and cart passed in a cloud of dust, and tried to remember the good days before Rhoda had come into her life. It was difficult. She could recall only tiny, coloured fragments from the life she and Dad had lived together, like looking into a kaleidoscope. Christmases. Birth-days. Days at the seaside. Otherwise, where ordinary day-to-day events were concerned, it was as though Rhoda had always been there. Yet Elvira, whose own mother had died giving birth to her, had been seven years old when her father had married Rhoda. He had met her in Yorkshire when he had gone up to attend to some business for Gran and Granfer Preston. Rhoda had been a housemaid at the farm where Granfer worked.

"You'll love her," Dad had promised Elvira. "You two'll get on wonderful well. I just know it!"

And at first it had been all right. Elvira had enjoyed coming home from school to find a fire lit and her dinner cooking, and having Rhoda read to her at bedtime and kiss her 'good-night', before she blew out the candle.

But then, almost imperceptibly at first, everything had started to change. The War had come, for one thing, and though it didn't seem to have much to do with Frissington Angel or the Prestons for a while, it had taken Dad away eventually. And just before Dad had left Arthur had been born . . . an unlovely, red-faced scrap of a baby, whose arrival had nevertheless sent Dad into ecstasies.

"To think I've got a son!" he had kept repeating on that June morning. "To think I've got a son!"

And it had seemed to Elvira that a door had slammed, leaving her on one side of it and Dad, Rhoda and Arthur on the other. Ever since then she had been uncomfortably aware of being the odd one out. During the evenings of her dad's short leaves, for example, after Rhoda had settled Arthur in his cot for the night, Elvira would begin to feel awkward, as though she were intruding on the couple. And when Dad was away, Rhoda's every care was for Arthur. How cold he was. How hungry. How tired. How happy or unhappy. And though she conscientiously saw that her stepdaughter was well-fed and well-clothed, it was out of a sense of duty rather than love. In fact in recent months it had seemed that Elvira was beginning to irritate Rhoda more and more. Elvira sucked on the end of one of the square goosegrass stems.

Perhaps she wants me out of the cottage, she mused. Wants me to go into service so that Arthur can have a room to himself. I wouldn't be surprised.

It was in the midst of these reflections that Elvira happened to glance to the right and saw the trackway for the first time. About a cart's width, it ran in a dead straight line between the slender poles of birch and hazel, and if Elvira hadn't been taught by her dad how to use her eyes, she might have thought it merely a woodland thoroughfare, made by the men who sometimes came to thin the coppice. As it was, though, she saw immediately that the track hadn't been beaten out by feet or traffic. It was clearly defined because the grass and the wild plants that covered it were stunted and withered by the drought, whereas the woodland undergrowth on either side of it was still green. Her father had often explained to her the reason for this type of irregularity in fields of corn or grass.

"That means stone or brick under there," he had told her.

16

"A buried roadway or sometimes a wall. For when there's drought the plants that grow atop rubble or mortar can't sink their roots down, you see, to find moisture, So they're stunted and parched-looking, poor, little old things!"

Elvira rose slowly to her feet, cradling the goosegrass in her pinafore. A stony roadway running through a coppice? It seemed most unlikely. Yet all the signs were there according to what Dad had told her. A few steps to her right and Elvira was in the coppice standing on the track. She began to move along it, uncertainly at first, but then more confidently as she saw that it ended about fifty yards ahead in what looked to be an open meadow. All at once, and for no definable reason Elvira was aware of, she felt a pleasurable little heart-flutter of antici-pation. She could hear unseen birds moving and settling in the branches above her head and a baby rabbit hopped unhurriedly across her path. From far away, in some peaceful field, floated the melodious plaints and responses of lambs and ewes.

She stopped for a moment, scarcely breathing lest she break the enchantment. The magic of the coppice was powerful. The green twilight. The scuttlings of tiny, invisible creatures. The scents of growing things. The sense of being benignly pro-tected by the tall, slender tree-sentinels. Then the more power-ful magnet of her curiosity drew her on again to the archway of golden light where green stalks, vibrant as sea-waves, were rippling in the light evening breeze. She emerged at last into the open, hardly knowing what she expected to find on this other side of the coppice — certainly not what she did find, that had her eyes round with wonder and her breath catching in her throat!

For there was an apple tree, ancient and gnarled, but still decked in a sprinkling of white blossom — and not far from it a well, its windlass and part of its circular brick wall just visible above a profusion of nettles. Then fragments of an old garden fence poking up above the greenery and still managing to confine a riot of deep mauve and vermilion where lilacs and rhododendrons ran amok and threatened to pour out into the meadow. But at the heart of it all lay the supreme wonder: a two-storeyed red brick house with a lean-to at one side, a quarter of its tiled roof gone, as though untidily pecked out by some gigantic bird! A house, solitary and uninhabited, with cobwebbed windows, cracked or glassless, and a front door that tapped in the breeze like a thoughtful finger. A secret, unexpected house whose existence had never been dreamed of by Elvira.

With a dry mouth and drumming heart that she normally associated with birthdays or with Christmas morning, Elvira followed the buried cart-track across the rough meadow to what must once have been the gateway of the house. Then she ploughed through knee-high buttercups and thistles to the front door. When she pushed it yielded only a little way, but left a gap wide enough for her to slip through. She found herself in a hallway, with a staircase straight ahead of her and a door opening on either side. A rusty iron footscraper, in the shape of a prowling cat, lay on its side on the brick floor, preventing the door from opening further.

After a moment's hesitation Elvira moved towards the inner door on her right. It wasn't properly closed, but its wood was warped and swollen and it gave way before her shoulder with a rheumaticky groan. The room she walked into was spacious with a window back and front, an open fireplace in the wall ahead of her, and to its right, a door leading into the lean-to scullery. The setting sun was slanting through the front window, making a narrow, golden river across the floor.

Elvira walked to the centre of the room and turned round once very slowly. Though the house was deserted there was no feeling of desolation about it. Indeed it was almost as though it were welcoming her like a lonely old person who's been waiting for company. She began to giggle gently, feeling herself tremble a little as she always did when she was happy and excited.

"Oh, yes!" she whispered, tiptoeing to look out at the wild glory of the lilacs and rhododendrons in the front garden. "You'll do, old house! You'll do. Just as good as any old smugglers' cave, you are! Better, I reckon!"

And she dropped her sheaf of goosegrass on to the floor and prepared to make a proper inspection of her tumbledown sanctuary.

4

The Sanctuary

In the scullery there was a grey sink beneath an unbroken but grime-encrusted window, a heap of bricks in one corner which had once supported a copper, and an ancient range backing on to the fireplace in the room which Elvira had just left. In the back wall a warped door stood permanently ajar, revealing a square pantry with a couple of shelves still in place and rusty hooks projecting down from the cobwebbed ceiling. To the left of the sink another, much sturdier door led into the garden. This was locked and bolted and all along the bottom were small, roughly circular holes gnawed out by generations of mice and rats whose droppings were visible all over the floor. Indeed, as Elvira stood there, silent and motionless, she could hear squeaks and scrapings from the interior of the old range and guessed that it must be a favourite nesting-place. The occasional mouse ventured into even the Prestons' gleaming, black-polished range to be lured out to its doom by one of the loathsome traps which Rhoda kept in every room.

"I won't do that," Elvira promised the scullery's invisible occupants. "Live and let live!"

That was what Miss Allison had always told them. "There's no deliberate malice in any of God's little creatures," she used to say. "They only do as nature dictates. So we should tolerate them as far as we possibly can."

Not that many people in the Frissingtons followed that dictum, Elvira thought wryly, as she crossed back through the front room and out into the hall again. Many men and boys seemed to spend half their lives trapping and killing. Rats and mice. Moles and sparrows. Rabbits and hares. Pheasants too when the keeper's back was turned. And occasionally a hunt went galloping through after foxes, or sometimes on foot when the otters down in the rivers were their quarry. That had really incensed Miss Allison. Indeed when the chairman of the managers had once called in to invite the whole school to come and watch the meet outside the Tumbledown Dick, she had informed him that neither she nor her pupils were interested in seeing barbarians in pink coats . . . a remark which apparently soon had the school managers after Miss Allison's blood, instead of the fox's!

Elvira crossed by the foot of the stairs and pushed the door facing her. It opened into what she guessed must have been the parlour. A pane of glass was missing from the front window and there were birds' droppings and feathers littering the floor. The hearthstone opposite the door had been gouged out and the surround of the fireplace ripped away leaving uneven hollows of rough mortar. Disfigured as it was the room was by no means intimidating because it was also gilded by the evening sun, and the fragrance of lilacs drifted in through the open window. Elvira could imagine it benevolently providing shelter for hapless little birds overtaken by blizzards or winter downpours. To the left of the fireplace a cupboard was built into the wall, but either it was locked or the door had jammed too tightly shut for it to yield even to her most strenuous tugging. She soon abandoned her efforts and went out to inspect the staircase.

Elvira was fully aware of the hazards involved in climbing a wooden stair in a building that was partly derelict. An insatiable bookworm, she devoured anything in print, including the newspaper which Rhoda brought home on Fridays and which specialized in detailed and colourful reports of accidents and fatalities. So she was familiar with accounts of reckless children who had fallen through the rotten floorboards of disused mills or factories and she was determined not to follow suit. Before mounting each step, therefore, she banged hard with the heel of her right boot along the whole length of the tread in order to find any weak spot. The effect was startling. Not only did her heel break clean through the pulpy wood at several points, but the whole building seemed to come suddenly alive. There was noise and movement everywhere: above her head, in the walls, beneath her feet. Patterings. Rushings. Scufflings. Squeaks. An occasional flutter of wings.

"It's all right. It's only me," she called out reassuringly. And her voice echoed around the small landing that was lit by a square, cobweb-curtained window. There was an immediate, profound hush, and Elvira was torn between giggling laughter and remorse, for she suddenly had a comical vision of hundreds of diamond eyes, twitching noses, whisking tails and scrabbling claws frozen into immobility, their owners crouching petrified in the dark netherworld that was their home.

"Poor, little old things!" she mumbled, half-ashamed for having enjoyed the fleeting sense of power the breathless silence gave her.

As she pushed open the door to her right into a room that ran the breadth of the house, a hard ball of fear gathered in her throat and the strength ebbed from her legs at the sight of a shadowy, motionless figure standing opposite her!

A couple of blood-chilling moments passed before Elvira realized she was looking into a dust-caked, full-length mirror that was propped against the wall facing her. And then relief made her so gay that she forgot all her previous precautions and ran headlong into the room across a wooden floor which fortunately proved sound. With the hem of her dark brown skirt she rubbed at the tarnished glass until, when she took a pace back, she could see her reflection fairly clearly. Elvira didn't often look at herself in a glass. For one thing, the only mirror in the Preston household was on the wardrobe in Rhoda's room where Elvira rarely lingered. For another, she didn't much like how she looked. Her face especially displeased her. She always looked peaky in the winter, even if she was as fit as a fiddle, and in the summer she turned gypsy-brown. And her eyebrows were too thick — like dark brown caterpillars, that malicious Sophie Christmas had told her once. And her nose was ridiculously small.

This evening, though, there was something different about

21

her appearance. Something which, at first, she couldn't quite pinpoint. Her clothes were the same as always so what had altered her? It was on encountering her reflection afresh, after a brief pirouette to scrutinize the remainder of the bare room, that she hit on it. For once she looked bright and alert. Almost — dare she even think it? — vivacious. It had always been Elvira's dream to look vivacious.

This place suits me, she thought, with a little lift of the heart. I reckon that's what it is. It agrees with me. Like the sea air agrees with some folks.

She did no more than peep into the two smaller rooms on the other side of the landing, for it was above these that the roof was bare of slates, and the woodwork in both of them was in a visibly poor condition. "Out of bounds!" she admonished herself in a gruff imitation of Mr Christmas, then she made her way cautiously back downstairs.

By the time Elvira had arrived back in the room where she had left her goosegrass, she knew for certain what she was going to do. The idea had been bubbling and fermenting in her head ever since she had walked through the front door. Now it had been strained and casked, as it were, and she could recognize it for what it was — 'the genuine article'. That's what Dad used to say about the home-brewed ale he made before harvest every year. "Nothing could be righter," he would grin, as he sampled a mouthful. And that's how it was with Elvira's decision. On the surface it might appear a childish prank. But it wasn't. She was in deadly earnest. She was going to leave home and come up here to live. Hide out, just as Ivy had done in her smugglers' cave, until the War was over, and her dad and Miss Allison had returned. Rhoda wouldn't grieve. Elvira was sure of that. She would leave her stepmother a note, of course, telling her not to worry, that she was safe and could look after herself. And Rhoda would probably give up her job and stay at home to look after Arthur, which would make her a lot happier. But meanwhile . . .

Meanwhile, Elvira thought excitedly, there was a lot of planning to do. She was going to have to make the house habitable, think about food-supplies, water and warmth. The main thing, of course, was to guard the secret of the house's existence. For none of her friends or schoolmates knew about it. She was sure of that. And if their parents did, they had either forgotten about it or thought it a matter of no importance. That was understandable, she reflected, since the house wasn't visible from the road and she could not remember the coppice in front of the house ever being thinned.

Despite the need for secrecy she was going to take one person into her confidence – someone who might be glad of a refuge – away from Miss Flint, and the Spartan routine of the home, and the humiliations imposed by Mr Christmas. Yes, if Clarry could be persuaded to come to the sanctuary it would be perfect, Elvira decided, as she lifted her goosegrass and slipped out of the front door. As she hurried across to the coppice to get home before the sun set, she suddenly realized, that she had inadvertently given the house a name: 'the Sanctuary'. She paused to look back at it before she entered the belt of trees. The wild garden looked quite beautiful, the shapes and shades of the lilacs and rhododendrons distinct and vivid in the limpid light of late evening. Behind them stood the house, looking benign and slightly regretful, like an old friend who was sorry to see her leave.

5

Of Ration-books and Spies

The next morning Rhoda was in a good humour, probably — Elvira decided — because it was pay day and she would be able to add to the nest egg she was accumulating. Rhoda's ambition was to leave Frissington Angel and move to Bingham Market where Tom Preston, on his return, could set up in business as a farrier and they could all live 'more civilized', as she put it. Sometimes Elvira contemplated this proposed move with happy anticipation, since Bingham Market possessed, amongst other attractions, a lending library, a railway station and a daily motorbus service to Ipswich.

At other times Frissington Angel staked an irrefutable claim to her affections, sending invisible tendrils twining around her heart to anchor her to her birthplace. It worked its magic this morning as she ran across the green at seven o'clock to fetch the milk from Mitchell's farm, leaving a trail of footprints behind her on the dewy grass. Cottages which normally looked ramshackle and unlovely were transfigured in the soft light and expectant hush of early morning. A spiral of smoke rose from Mr Diaper's forge, aiming for an eggshell-blue sky. And away to the right the church tower, four square and sturdy, stood guard over all.

In the farm dairy, Mrs Mitchell, ruddy-cheeked and buxom, ladled the skimmed milk into Elvira's quart-can, while behind an inner door the separator hummed, saving the cream that would later be churned into butter.

"Sixpence, my love," the farmer's wife said, and her podgy red hand opened to swallow the small silver coin.

"Sixpence for a quart of milk!" Rhoda sighed, as she spooned Quaker oats from the cooking-pot into two dishes. "It's wicked! Hardly seems yesterday since it was twopence. Just as well I'm earning, Elvie! Else we couldn't afford to eat."

Elvira nodded, cutting herself a slice of bread and spreading it thinly with margarine. Then she walked over to the range to make the tea and brought the big brown teapot back to sit in the centre of the table.

"It's a shame Mr Mitchell had to sell his herd," she remarked between mouthfuls. "Seems funny them only having five cows and all that big cattle yard."

Rhoda poured two cups of tea. "Couldn't do much else, poor man!" she replied. "What with the War Committee taking all his grazing away and ploughing it up. That was his field along the St Peter road, wasn't it?" she added. "The one just before that coppice . . . where they burned the hedges?"

"Mmm." Elvira sounded as unconcerned as possible, fuming inwardly at her own blundering stupidity. For the last place she wished to discuss with Rhoda (or with anyone else, for that matter) was her goosegrass field and its vicinity, since there was always the danger that she might resurrect the memory of the derelict house in someone's mind. She must be more careful in future, she resolved, much more careful!

"I'll go up and fetch Artie now," she mumbled, hastily swallowing the remainder of her tea and making for a door to the left of the fireplace which concealed the steep little staircase.

Rhoda had to leave at seven-thirty to walk down to Frissington St Peter and catch the factory-truck, while Elvira was left to wash, clothe and feed little Arthur, before handing him over to Mrs Boniface at half-past-eight. Despite the fact that Arthur had only bread and milk with a sprinkling of sugar for breakfast, feeding him could be a tedious business. This morning, for example, Elvira was forced to guide his small spoon to his mouth, with, "A little drop for Tommy, the horse," and, "One for the Boniface kitty," and a spoonful for every other furred or feathered creature of Arthur's acquaintance. The result was that she was late in leaving for school, arriving with her goosegrass just in time for registration, and having no opportunity to exchange even a word with Clarry.

At morning break, before they could leave their seats, Miss Gray, the pupil-teacher who had been weighing the bundles of goosegrass, arrived to pay the contributors.

"So! Our Elvira did manage to overcome her insuperable difficulties after all!" Mr Christmas remarked caustically, rocking to and fro on his heels as a fiery-cheeked Elvira was given her farthing.

"More than Sophie Christmas did!" Ethel Foster, Elvira's neighbour mumbled, her mouth full of bread and jam. "Says she had a migraine, poor, delicate, little flower!"

Mr Christmas, overhearing his grand-daughter's name, was frowning at Ethel admonishingly when the classroom door suddenly burst open, and the Rector of Frissington St Peter strode in.

The Reverend Robson-Turner was a tall, thin, pleasant man,

and because he suffered from asthma and was slightly stooped, Elvira had once thought of him as being almost elderly. Rhoda, however, had informed her that he wasn't above thirty-five and that he would be an excellent husband for Miss Allison who always went pink when he spoke to her. Mr Christmas didn't go pink, but he did look rather put out at the unexpected interruption, especially when the children scuffled to their feet for the visitor, the girls making their customary curtseys and the boys saluting.

The Reverend Robson-Turner, brandishing a printed form, beamed round the room and nodded to the children to resume their seats.

"Application form for the new ration-books," he explained to the headmaster. "Must be in by June 6th — next Thursday. Promised I'd explain to the children how to fill it in so they can assist their parents. Clean forgot! Head like a sieve nowadays. Holier and holier!" His smile became truly radiant at his inadvertent pun and some of the sharper children tittered appreciatively.

Miss Gray, cued by Mr Christmas, grabbed a pile of scrap-paper from the cupboard and started to pass it around. As the rector's neat printing advanced down the blackboard, Elvira copied along with the others even though she knew what Rhoda's reaction would be.

"They must think I'm half daft or something!" she had declared crossly, when a much younger Elvira had dutifully started to show her how to apply for her registration card. "I can read and write, you know! My brain hasn't wholly rusted up, even though I do live in Frissington Angel. You can go back and tell them that!"

Elvira hadn't understood Rhoda's indignation. After all, neither Lizzie Pitt's nor Ethel Foster's mothers could read, and they were more than grateful to have their children help them with forms. Now, however, Elvira realized that Rhoda's pride had been hurt, that she didn't want to be thought of as an 'angel', the local nickname for a Frissington Angel woman. Rhoda was an incomer and thought herself superior to women like Mrs Pitt who had to take in washing and work in the fields singling beet or stone picking to help bring up her family. She had even refused to go gleaning for corn for the hens last autumn, though she had been glad enough of what Elvira brought home. In fact, Elvira decided, Rhoda was probably just as uppity as Sophie Christmas who, sitting two rows in front, was showing that she had no need to copy from the board by yawning pointedly. Sophie, who was only ten but bright enough to be in Standard 5, had come to Frissington St Peter a year ago with Mr Christmas and his wife, because there had been bombing near her Essex boarding school. She made no secret of her contempt for the little 'clod-hoppers' with whom she now had to mix.

"I'm not allowed even to walk up to Frissington Angel," she had informed Elvira not long after her arrival. "Gran says it's a rural slum full of roughnecks."

"Well! The nasty old crow!" Rhoda had exploded, when Elvira had passed on this piece of information. "What does she think the Christmases are? Royalty or something?"

Unfortunately there were those in Frissington St Peter who treated the headmaster and his family as though they were exactly that, Elvira thought sourly. Mrs Fisher, the shop-keeper, for instance. Sophie was often to be seen perched on the stool at the end of her counter, talking non-stop in her piercing little voice ("Mardling on like a right old woman," as Lizzie Pitt contemptuously described it), while Mrs Fisher, ingratiatingly offered her a toffee.

A hand fell on Elvira's shoulder and she jumped guiltily as she looked up, expecting to find Mr Christmas's gimlet-eyes boring into her. Instead she encountered the rector's benevolent smile.

"Still working your way along Miss Allison's bookshelves, Elvira?" he whispered. "Have you tackled my friend Dickens, yet? You were heading in his direction just before Miss Allison left."

Elvira's face flushed. "No sir," she murmured. "It's a bit difficult, like," she added vaguely, and glanced, without thinking, in the headmaster's direction.

The rector frowned and bent low to speak very softly into Elvira's ear. "You still have access to Miss Allison's books in the schoolhouse, I hope," he muttered. "She specifically left instructions." Elvira shook her head, feeling her face grow hotter as her classmates began to notice she had been singled out for the rector's attention.

"I did ask about it once," she replied at last in a faltering whisper. "But they said I must have been mistaken — that Miss Allison's books were all locked away."

The rector straightened with a 'tut-tut' of annoyance. Then, having enquired after Lizzie Pitt's mother and Flora Crack's new baby brother, Kitchener, he gave a curt nod in Mr Christmas's direction and left.

"What was the old rector jawing to you about?" Clarry enquired at lunch-break when he and Elvira were settled in their favourite spot — an angle of the school wall which was overshadowed by an oak of impressive girth.

"Oh, nothing important," she replied, delving into her lunch-bag, and watching with widening eyes as Clarry pulled out a single, hard-looking bun from his.

"That all you've got to eat, then?" she demanded, watching Clarry attack the bun ravenously.

The boy nodded. "Says she's run out of things again. Reckons we're eating more than our rations."

Elvira slid a thick, dripping sandwich on to Clarry's knee. "Take that," she told him. "I brought it special . . . just in case." And as his broad grin almost split his thin face in two, she added abruptly, "How would you like to get away from old Flintstones, Clarry? And from old Happy Christmas, too? Hide up for a while? Look after ourselves? Reckon I've found just the place."

Clarry was chewing slowly and with relish, his sharp, grey eyes never moving from Elvira's face. Finally he paused for long enough to enquire, "No joking, Elvie?"

"No joking!" she assured him almost fiercely. Then added, "I could take you there tomorrow afternoon, Clarry. Then you'll see with your own eyes!"

But Clarry was shaking his head. "Not Saturday," he mumbled, still chewing. "Have to work on the allotment. Sunday'd do. Afternoon?"

"Two o'clock . . . I'll come to your gate," Elvira agreed hurriedly, as she noticed a gang of Clarry's cronies racing across the yard towards them.

"Aeroplane!" the leader was yelling. "Aeroplane's landed on Church Meadow, Clarry! Coming to see it?" As the crowd of boys circled and made for the yard gate, Clarry snatched up his dinner-bag and shot off after them. Elvira shook her head. Honestly! Aeroplanes were always landing on Church Meadow. It was to do with training the pilots, Rhoda said. But the boys never failed to break bounds to run around and gape at them. And they always ended up in hot water with silly, big Clarry being made the scapegoat for the whole bunch.

"I know something you don't, Elvira Preston!" Elvira winced. There was no mistaking the high-pitched, imperious voice of Sophie Christmas. And, even as Elvira wondered whether she could make a bolt for it, the red-haired girl planted herself square in front of her, blocking any escape route. Elvira had now progressed to a slice of the date cake that Rhoda had brought home from Ipswich last Tuesday and she was determined to enjoy it to the full. So she stared mutely ahead, completely ignoring the smug-looking Sophie in her cool, blue blouse, white socks and summer shoes.

"I'll tell you about it, if you like," Sophie declared, having endured Elvira's aloof silence for a minute. Unable to contain herself any longer, she burst out with, "An army motor stopped outside the post office this morning, and four soldiers got out, and Mrs Fisher says they're after a spy because someone's been transmitting wireless messages to the enemy!"

"A spy! In the Frissingtons!" Elvira's hilarious incredulity overcame even her disinclination to talk to Sophie Christmas. "Going to tell the old Huns how much clover Mr Spurgeon's cut this year, are they? Or how Mr Diaper got kicked by the old stallion last week?"

29

"Laugh if you like!" Sophie exclaimed, her freckled face shooting forward as she stamped her foot. "But we've got Huns in Frissington St Peter already, don't forget! Wandering about all over the place. And walls have ears, Mrs Fisher says! And there's those that work in the aircraft factory might open their mouths too much. Like your mother, for instance!"

"Well, not in Mrs Fisher's shop: that's for certain!" Elvira snapped back, thoroughly ruffled now. "Rhoda won't set foot in there, and I don't wonder, either! Proper gossip-shop that is nowadays. Not to mention the little pig with big ears that's always stuck up in the corner!" she finished with a toss of her head as she flounced off to join Flora Crack and Ethel Foster who were strolling slowly, arms linked, across the yard.

"Well, I'm going to look out for the spy anyway!" Sophie's insistent voice pursued her. "It's our duty. Everyone's duty. Mrs Fisher says so. And so does Grandpa!"

"She's got spy-mania, that Mrs Fisher!" Rhoda exclaimed that evening when Elvira told her of the incident. "She's had a bee in her bonnet ever since they brought those prisoners here. Proper old Hun-hater she is, and no mistake!"

Elvira was sitting with Arthur on her knee by the window, and for some reason she remembered the incident of the syrup-tin car. "Dad says there's lots of them just ordinary folks like us," she remarked dreamily.

Rhoda, not listening properly, said, "If only a letter would come from him! Gets on your nerves this waiting day after day, even though they do say no news is good news! I've got his next parcel all ready to send now with one of those fancy electric torches in it. But I can't be sure he's still in the same place. Not with the Germans advancing like they are."

Little Arthur, growing sleepy, wriggled out of Elvira's arms and ran over to crawl up on his mother. Rhoda, clasping him in her arms, started to hum softly and soon the two shapes in the shadow-filled corner merged into one.

Oh, no! There was no fear that she would ever be missed by these two, Elvira thought enviously as she watched them. In fact she reckoned they would hardly even notice that she'd gone.

6

Buckets and Books

At the best of times Elvira disliked Saturday mornings because her main task of the day was to fill the outhouse copper with pails of water from the well behind the Six Bells pub on the other side of the green. This was so that Rhoda, who worked until midday, could attack the weekly wash straight after dinner. On this particular Saturday, with the sun already glaring heartlessly down by nine o'clock, the prospect of several dusty treks down to the Frissington St Peter pump plunged Elvira into the blackest gloom.

"Artie play wif Rosie Cooper?" her little brother enquired, making hideous grimaces as Elvira rubbed his face with a wet cloth.

"No. Not this morning," Elvira told him. "We'll have to ask if Mrs Honeyball'll see after you. Rosie's got measles."

Arthur pushed away the piece of ragged towel with which Elvira was drying him. He'd been cross-grained ever since waking and now he was spoiling for a fight.

"Artie want one, too," he stated, his blue eyes gleaming acquisitively. "Artie want a measle."

"Well, Artie can't have one!" Elvira retorted snappily, raising her eyes to heaven as the first heartrending wails issued from Arthur's gaping mouth. Even fat, easygoing Mrs Honeyball might look askance if this noisy, purple-faced creature were dropped on her doorstep!

Mrs Honeyball, however, with four raucous youngsters of her own, took Arthur in her stride when Elvira presented him, still roaring, five minutes later.

"Do you stop that blaring!" she bellowed, on an even more ear-splitting note than Arthur's. "And get yourself indoors to play with our Mary-Anne. She can't abide none of her own brothers this morning." Then as Arthur, miraculously silenced, toddled into what Rhoda contemptuously referred to as "Ivy Honeyball's pandemonium" the woman put a red,

31

podgy hand on Elvira's shoulder. "And do you go careful, now, Elvie love," she whispered dramatically, " 'cos fares like we've got a German spy right here in the Frissingtons, sending signals out to the enemy and all that! That's all round the parish, so it must be true!"

"Rhoda reckons that's just Mrs Fisher's imagination," Elvira replied, then wished she hadn't spoken because Mrs Honeyball looked so crestfallen.

"Maybe so," the latter admitted grudgingly after a moment. "But Mr Honeyball believes it, Elvie. And he's no fool! Your dad could vouch for that."

Elvira nodded a hasty agreement. Lame Mr Honeyball was head horsekeeper at Mitchell's farm and was renowned for his skill with Suffolks.

"Anyway," Mrs Honeyball went on, cheering up again, "that's just reminded me, Elvie. Mr Honeyball left something for you." She disappeared round the corner of the cottage, silencing a squabble en route, and came back holding a wooden yoke with an empty bucket dangling from each end. "Real old-fashioned contraption!" she declared. "But that's worth its weight in gold this weather. Mr Honeyball says you can borrow it any time you want, your being Tom's gel." While she talked she settled the padded yoke comfortably across Elvira's shoulders and stood back to admire it. "Cor!" she exclaimed. "You look just like one of those pretty nut-brown dairymaids in a picture book, Elvira! And that's the truth."

In fact Elvira felt only abysmally foolish as she set off on her first journey down to the pump and she fully intended to return the yoke as soon as she could on the pretext that she found it too uncomfortable. Soon, however, as she realized how much ground she was effortlessly covering on her return journey, she changed her mind. Indeed, she wouldn't have parted with the yoke had everyone in the Frissingtons come to jeer at her! As it was, of all the market-goers who passed her by in traps, carts or on bicycles, not one of them gave Elvira a second glance.

"People have more to think about!" Rhoda would always say, if Elvira ever worried about attracting attention. And that was probably true, Elvira reflected as she swung downhill for her third load. No doubt this morning they would be worrying about the German victories. Or about getting their new ration-books. Perhaps even about the Frissington spy!

Elvira's brow wrinkled as she looked around her at the familiar landscape, at the fields of barley and wheat rolling gently down to the little river on her left. At the coppice on her right with the goosegrass-path up which she would take Clarry tomorrow to inspect the Sanctuary. What could a spy possibly find here that would be of the slightest interest to the Huns? Then, almost immediately, she remembered Sophie Christmas's remark about the local women who worked in the aircraft factory. Yes . . . that was true, she allowed. A lot of the Frissington women worked there now. And doubtless the Germans would very much like to know what was going on inside that factory. But on the other hand, if any of the aircraft-workers did talk (which was unlikely since they were all sworn to secrecy about their production-figures and things) how on earth could a spy conceal himself so as to overhear them? Everyone in the Frissingtons knew everyone else after all! And most of their business, too!

At that precise moment Elvira's eye fell on the high brick wall to her right, with its ugly trimming of barbed wire, and she remembered the prisoners. How full of hatred they must be, she reflected, feeling a sudden thrust of fear! Caged in there like ferrets and only allowed out to work for their captors. Could any of them possibly hate the Frissingtons enough to want to destroy them? To bring those planes they called 'Gothas' over here to drop bombs. Or, even worse, to bring Zeppelins!

Elvira was more afraid of Zeppelins than of anything in the world. Not that she had ever seen one, except in her nightmares — nightmares which had started soon after Mr Christmas had described in great detail a Zeppelin raid he had experienced at Southend. Longer than a football-pitch, he had

33

sworn that German airship was! And making a noise like a hundred railway trains as it hovered above dropping its deadly cargo! Even now in the heat of the morning Elvira came out in an icy sweat as she thought of it and a great shuddering sigh escaped her. Then suddenly, she squared her shoulders and marched on again, setting the empty buckets swinging jauntily. "Never cross your bridges!" her dad was always telling her. And anyway the thought of a Zeppelin wasting its bombs on the sleepy little Frissingtons was absurd! The heat must be affecting her brain, she told herself contemptuously. Or else she'd caught spy-fever like silly Mrs Fisher!

Elvira was to hear more about spy-fever that afternoon. For her day, with its unpromising start, was to hold an unexpected treat.

"Tell you what, Elvie," Rhoda said that lunchtime, as she shoved a final spoonful of mince into a reluctant Arthur. "I think I ought to put a book into that parcel of your dad's. I forgot last time and you know what a reader he is!"

Elvira, who had been daydreaming about the Sanctuary, returned with a start to give a hasty nod.

"Well, then," Rhoda went on, lifting Arthur down from the table. "How about you going in to Mr Robertson's in Bingham Market for me this afternoon? You'll have to walk there, but I'll give you the money to come home with the carrier. Your dad swears by Mr Robertson for a good second-hand book."

"Oh, yes!" Elvira, face alight, was already flying outside to wipe her face and hands so that she could be on her way.

She was given a lift twice along the five miles between Frissington St Peter and Bingham Market: first by Mrs Spurgeon the farmer's wife who was going in her trap to visit her sister, two miles along the road, and then by Mr Diaper, the blacksmith who hoisted Elvira up into his rattly, old cart for the last mile of her journey.

"Not that I would have minded walking every inch of the way!" she reflected happily as Bingham Market church tower came in sight. "Not when I'm going to see Mr Robertson and his books! This really has been a good day. First Mr Honeyball's yoke and now the bookshop!"

Once inside the poky little bookshop with its bursting shelves Elvira was lost to the world. She floated happily along the rows, hovering, then pouncing on unknown authors, noting promising names for future reference. Not that she could afford to buy any of the books. For books were special luxuries given at birthdays and Christmas time. But Mr Robertson allowed her to browse to her heart's content.

"Here you are, Elvira. This should suit your dad." Mr Robertson, brandishing a book, emerged suddenly from the cubbyhole that was the back shop. He was a wiry, little Scotsman with a straggly, white beard and sparkling, blue eyes. "It's called *The Riddle of the Sands*," he informed her. "By an Irish writer called Childers. Tom'll enjoy it."

Elvira opened the book doubtfully. She thought it sounded dry and Rhoda had specifically instructed her not to choose a dry book. Then she saw the subtitle: *A Record of Secret Service*, and her face cleared.

"Exciting, is it, Mr Robertson?" she asked eagerly. "About spies?"

"Aye. It is, I suppose," he agreed. "About two young English spies in North Germany."

"Do you think there are any German spies in Suffolk, Mr Robertson?" Elvira enquiried conversationally, as she counted six coppers out into the man's hand.

The bookseller's reaction was totally unexpected, for his face flamed and his blue eyes glinted angrily beneath his white, bushy brows. "No, I do not!" he snapped. "And the least said about that the better as far as I'm concerned!" Then, seeing Elvira look startled, he put his arm around her shoulders and guided her gently to the window. "Look over there, my dear," he directed, nodding towards the other side of the square, clearly visible now through market-stalls that had diminished to a mere handful since the beginning of the War. "Can you see Mr Price's shop?"

"Oh, yes!" Elvira gasped, noticing for the first time the

rough boards nailed across what had been the jeweller's shining plate-glass window, and the letters whitewashed across the door.

"Filthy Hun," Mr Robertson read out bitterly. "And a more honest, generous, old fellow never lived. They did that last night, Elvira. They broke the glass and the old man's heart at the same time."

"But why?" Elvira demanded, staring up at Mr Robertson. "Mr Price isn't a German, is he?"

"No. But some busybody poked and pried and discovered that the old chap's great-grandfather came over here from Germany in 1785. And that's the result! Witch-hunting! It's wicked, Elvira," he added, turning away with a sigh. "Don't ever have any part of it. Your dad would tell you the same, if he were here. I know he would."

All at once Elvira was painfully aware of just how much she was missing her dad, with his funny old Suffolk sayings, and his fiery outbursts about things like justice and men's rights.

"We haven't heard from Dad for ever so long, Mr Robertson!" she brought out a shade tremulously. "Not for over four weeks. Rhoda's getting ever so worried."

"Oh, I shouldn't think there's any need to worry. I believe things are all topsy-turvy at the Front at the moment. His letters have likely been delayed." Mr Robertson's head had shot round sharply. But his voice was matter-of-fact as he smiled reassuringly at Elvira. "This old War's bound to end soon, my pet," he went on. "And your dad'll be back here every Saturday night again, draining my teapot dry and quarrelling about politics. You'll see!"

Feeling cheered, Elvira started towards the door but Mr Robertson beckoned her back. "Hold on a minute, lass!" he commanded. "I've put a book aside for you over here. I've just remembered it." He reached up to the top shelf of his 'ordered' section and pulled down a brown, leather-bound book. "You'll maybe have it already?" he enquired tentatively, as Elvira's eager fingers grasped it.

But Elvira was shaking her head, her eyes glowing her

gratitude. For the book was *The Children of the New Forest* which Miss Allison had started to read to the older pupils just before she left, and which Mr Christmas had dismissed as being 'beyond their understanding'.

"Oh, I am glad Rhoda asked me to come today!" Elvira exclaimed, hugging the two books to her chest. "Thank you ever so, Mr Robertson!"

The bookseller gently told her that she was welcome. As Elvira finally opened the door, jerking the tinny, little bell into a querulous clamour, he called, "And don't be trying to read it along the road now! Or you'll be colliding with folk and falling over your feet like your dad does!"

Elvira nodded obediently, and succeeded in keeping the book unopened until she was safely seated on a hard plank in the comparative gloom of the carrier's covered cart. Then, despite strongly-voiced warnings from several of her fellow-passengers that she would be blind before her journey's end, she ceased to hear the rattle of the cart, or the women complaining because eggs were still selling at four pence a-piece, and she joined the orphaned Cavalier children as they learned to fend for themselves in their new woodland environment. The more she read, the more she marvelled at the happy accident that had landed this particular book in her lap just when she had stumbled upon the Sanctuary. For why shouldn't the coppice and its surroundings become a kind of New Forest for herself and Clarry? What was to prevent them living as securely and happily as the Beverley family in her book?

7

The Children of the Coppice

Sunday was hotter than ever. At ten o'clock Mr Diaper, the blacksmith, roared across to Rhoda (who was valiantly scraping with her hoe between the peas and broad beans in the rock-hard front garden) that the thermometer on his shed was already showing seventy-five degrees.

"Need we go to Sunday school today, Rhoda?" Elvira asked plaintively from the doorstep, where she was spinning a top for Arthur. Usually she didn't mind Sunday school, but this morning the lure of her new book, and the hideous prospect of the trek down to Frissington St Peter Congregational chapel, made her feel rebellious.

"Indeed you do!" Rhoda frowned, stopping to wipe the perspiration from her brow with the back of her hand. "It's your flower-and-egg day today, don't you forget! What would they all think if the Prestons stopped away?"

Elvira groaned aloud. She had forgotten that this was the Sunday on which the children were each expected to bring an egg and some flowers for the soldiers in local hospitals. But even if it hadn't been, she reflected sourly, Rhoda wouldn't have let them stay at home. For after Rhoda had seen Arthur and Elvira into the Sunday school at eleven, she and the other mothers would go back to one of their homes and sit talking and drinking tea until they went into their own chapel service at twelve. Elvira knew very well how much Rhoda looked forward to her little weekly news-session! But at least she and Arthur didn't have to go into the adult service too, Elvira thought, slowing the red, wooden top with her finger-tip until it began to wobble drunkenly. Some of the other children did and Elvira would have hated that. She even preferred trailing home alone with Arthur and laying the table for dinner, to spending another hour in the chapel. And there was no cooking to do. For since Rhoda had started working, Sunday dinner was always the same in the summertime. Cold ham, cold boiled potatoes, fresh vegetables, table jelly and fruit.

"Elvira Preston! You gone deaf or something?" Elvira, feeling her shoulder roughly shaken, looked up to find her stepmother frowning down on her in exasperation. "I've asked you twice to take Artie in and clean him up while I finish this," Rhoda exclaimed. "His clean frock's lying over the chair in the scullery. You are a great, dozy creature nowadays, Elvie! You really are!"

Elvira rose very slowly to her feet. She hated being man-handled by Rhoda. But she then reflected that she and Rhoda would soon be parting company, so a protest would be a waste of effort, especially on a hot day like this. She scooped Arthur up to carry him into the cottage, the thought of the Sanctuary now fluttering joyously inside her head, like the white butter-fly that had come to dance amongst Rhoda's beans.

Clarry had inspected the interior of the Sanctuary and the outhouses at the back. Now he was standing out in front of the house, knee-high in buttercups, shading his eyes and scanning the surrounding countryside like a lookout on a ship.

Straight ahead, and to the left, a curving strip of rough meadow about twenty yards wide, separated the 'garden' from the coppice. But to the right was wilder country, as yet unexplored. Clarry stared at the profusion of bramble bushes, each clinging to its neighbour as though to form an impenetrable barrier. Then he started prowling around in the buttercups, stooping occasionally, and finally coming up triumphantly with a rotting, wooden spar that had once formed part of the fence.

"Come on, Elvie!" he exhorted. "I want to see what there is over here." And he stalked off on his long legs to slash a path through the prickly bushes, with Elvira trotting in his wake. Almost immediately though, he stopped, and so suddenly that Elvira bumped into him. For a precarious moment they both wobbled on the edge of a large, circular depression, whose sides bristled with nettles and brambles. There were other similar, shallow pits farther along the slope and Elvira, having regained her breath and her balance, shook Clarry's arm excitedly.

"I know what this is!" she exclaimed. "It's the old brickfield! Dad's mentioned it once or twice, but I've never been here. This must be where they dug the clay out."

"And that's the back of the Old Factory down at the foot of the slope," Clarry stated. "You can just see the upper storey above the wall."

39

Elvira's eyes clouded. "Let's not go any further," she said quickly. "That place gives me the shivers. And anyway, we don't want to be spotted up here."

The boy nodded and two minutes later they were back in the security of the Sanctuary sitting cross-legged on the floor beneath the front window of the parlour. Elvira took a deep breath of the lilac perfume that was drifting in through the broken pane.

"Well, Clarry?" she said quietly. "What do you think? Could we do it? Live here?"

"Seems all right," Clarry said carefully. "Shouldn't think they'd find us at any rate. Real back of beyond up here." Then, chin on hand, he appeared to fall into a profound meditation. It was a full five minutes before he shot Elvira a sharp glance.

"What was you reckoning to do about food, then?" he queried. "And fuel? Things like that?"

Elvira's eyes shone. She was already halfway through *The Children of the New Forest* and she was bursting to give Clarry an account of how the Beverleys had managed — an example she was hoping they could follow. When she came to the end of her enthusiastic recital though, she couldn't help but notice the apprehension in Clarry's eyes.

"Don't you think we could do it, then?" she enquired anxiously.

"Not the hunting bit," Clarry retorted dismally. "Not making traps for animals and that. And even if I did, I couldn't eat them. That'd be like murder, Elvie. My stomach'd turn."

Elvira frowned. She hadn't reckoned on Clarry's sensitivity. But she understood it. Country-bred herself, she still couldn't bear to be near the harvest fields when they started killing the rabbits.

"Tell you what," she said brightly after a moment. "Suppose we had a couple of hens? We could sell their eggs at the market and buy our meat. How'd that be?"

"Where'd we get hens, then?" Clarry gaped. "And how'd we get to market without being spotted?"

"Oh, Clarry, for goodness' sake! Stop crossing your

40

bridges!" Elvira replied crossly. "We've plenty of time to think about details like that! For the moment we've to set about clearing the place up. The inside of the house has to be cleaned. The ground's to be got ready for planting. And that old well's to be unblocked. That's for a start! Now are you going to be my partner, or aren't you?"

" 'Course I am!" Clarry grinned happily. "What if I smuggle up a few brushes and pails and things whenever I get a chance? There's cupboards crammed with them in that rectory that old Flintstones has never even seen."

"Great!" Elvira said enthusiastically. "That's exactly the kind of thing we need, Clarry. I don't suppose you could manage a spade or a hoe?" she added doubtfully.

"No problem!" Clarry assured her. "The gardener's shed's full of them. They'll never be missed. 'S just a question of me getting up early in the morning. Old Flintstones is dead to the world till after eight."

"Well, if you do that, Clarry, we can start work next Sunday," Elvira informed him. "It's difficult for me to get out evenings. Though I might manage the odd time or two."

Clarry nodded, looking around him with narrowing eyes.

"Funny," he murmured. "Doesn't seem like a deserted house at all, somehow. It's got the feeling of being lived in. Know what I mean?"

"I felt it was friendly right from the start," Elvira said, standing up and brushing the dust from her skirt. "Can't wait to get started, can you Clarry? It'll be just like stepping into my book."

Clarry, standing up too, cleared a patch on the dusty window-pane and peered out into the sunlight.

" 'The Children of the Coppice'!" he spluttered suddenly, digging a bony elbow into Elvira's ribs. "That's what we'll be, Elvie. Think somebody'll write a story about us one day?"

"Far too much imagination! That's your trouble, Clarry Rae!" Elvira exclaimed with a long-suffering sigh, as she steered her friend firmly towards the door.

41

8

A Letter from France

Monday being the third of June and the king's birthday, Mr Christmas had decided, weeks before, that it would be a patriotic gesture to put on a display in the playground that morning after break. So despite the heat and the fact that Mrs Christmas was the sole spectator (the rector having popped in earlier to plead a pressing engagement) the children filed out into the playground at two minutes past eleven.

"Stupid! That's what it is!" Lizzie Pitt grumbled to Elvira. "Wasn't any hope of an audience today, was there? What with the haysel going on and it being washing-day and all!"

"Still — I don't suppose they could change the date of the king's birthday just to fit in with the washing." Elvira grinned. She was feeling more at peace with the world now that she had the dream of the Sanctuary to sustain her.

Ethel Foster was scowling darkly as Standards 5 and 6 were hustled along by Miss Gray to form a semi-circle in the half of the playground that was near to the road.

"Just so's that Sophie Christmas can recite *The Charge of the Light Brigade* for the umpteenth time!" she whispered vindictively over her shoulder to Elvira. "Wish I'd said my throat was sore and stopped at home."

There were several items on the programme before Sophie was due to perform. The Union Jack was run up and saluted. There was a very ragged rendering of *God Save the King* with the little ones still singing long after their seniors had finished. Sidney Spurgeon recited *Home Thoughts from the Sea* in an embarrassed, garbled fashion after which all eighty pupils marched round the yard to the strident singing of *Rule Britannia*. Then Mr Christmas, having debated with his wife as to whether it would be seemly for the pupils to sit on the ground on such an occasion, finally gave an affirmatory nod to Miss Gray, at the same time beckoning to Sophie to take her place in the centre of the circle.

"Here we go!" Ethel Foster sighed. "Frissington's answer to Cicely Courtneidge . . . Just look at her, Elvie, in that new pink blouse! All dressed up like the pig going to market."

Elvira, however, was looking curiously beyond Sophie and her grandfather, to where the tall, angular figure of Miss Penrose, the postmistress was hurrying across the playground from School Lane. And a moment later the postmistress's urgent, "I say! I say!" had Mr Christmas wheeling round, and every head turned in her direction.

"She's got a letter," Flora Crack whispered in Elvira's ear. "Looks like the kind my dad sends home from the Front."

"Must be important," Ethel Foster remarked. "They're having ever such a long jaw about it. It's even put a stop to the *Light Brigade*."

As they watched, Mr Christmas bent down to whisper something in his grand-daughter's ear and Sophie came flying, straight as an arrow, towards Elvira.

"Will you come over for a moment please, Elvira?" she asked, and something in Sophie's subdued manner, and in the formally polite tone of her voice made Elvira's stomach knot up with apprehension. She could feel every eye in the school fixed on her as she followed Sophie on trembling legs to the centre of the circle.

"Ah, Elvira!" Mr Christmas greeted her, and his voice, too, was uncharacteristically restrained. "Miss Penrose here has a little problem . . ." As the headmaster's voice tailed off unhelpfully the postmistress took over.

"It's this letter just come in for your stepmother, dear," she announced, waving the grey-blue envelope above Elvira's head. "From France it is. But not in your dad's handwriting. And I know how Rhoda's been waiting. So I thought we should try to get it to her right away."

"Yes," Elvira murmured, feeling suddenly sick in the pit of her stomach.

"We wondered if you could possibly take it to her," Mr Christmas put in, frowning down at Elvira doubtfully. "Any idea as to how you might get there? To the factory, I mean?"

43

Elvira shook her head.

"I have, though!" Sophie burst in, her eyes like goosegogs. "Dr Fletcher's surgery-boy is going into Ipswich at half-eleven on his motor-bicycle, Grandpa. I heard him tell Mrs Fisher in the shop. 'Spect he'd take Elvira on his carrier."

"I'm sure he would!" Mr Christmas exclaimed, beaming down on Sophie. "Bright as a button!" he remarked in a loud whisper to Miss Penrose. Then he turned back to Elvira. "Best race round to Dr Fletcher's straight away, my dear," he said. "Ask the good doctor's permission, of course, though I'm sure he won't object. Then hop on that infernal machine behind young Thomas Crow and you'll be at the factory in next to no time!"

"Yes, sir," Elvira whispered, turning obediently away.

"Don't forget the letter, dear! Here! Put it in that deep pocket in your skirt, then it'll be safe." Miss Penrose's bony hand fell comfortingly on Elvira's shoulder as she walked with her to the edge of the circle where two of the younger children silently made a space for the pair to pass through. "And it might not be bad news, Elvira," she added, in what was for her, a gentle voice. "So don't you be worrying yourself sick on the journey now. There's no point in crossing our bridges . . ."

"No. That's what Dad always says," Elvira agreed numbly.

As it turned out she had little time to think of anything except self-preservation during the thirty minutes of her motor-bicycle journey. She was perched precariously on a narrow, metal carrier with her feet resting on the back edge of Thomas's pedals and her arms clamped tightly around his middle. Added to this was the fact that Thomas, invalided out of the army at eighteen with two toes missing from each foot, was a speed-fiend who flew along any straight stretch of road at over twenty miles per hour, and who rarely dropped beneath fifteen even to negotiate a tricky bend. Chilled to the bone, since she was wearing no protection against the wind, bumped and bruised from the carrier and half suffocated with the dust they had kicked up, Elvira eventually fell, rather than dismounted, from her pillion-seat at the factory gate and stood dazed for a few moments, barely aware that Thomas was roaring on his way with a wave of farewell.

"Well, my love? And what can we do for you?" A man with one arm stepped out of the gatekeeper's 'sentry-box' behind the steel mesh of the closed gate and looked through enquiringly at Elvira. She tried to explain what her errand was, but the dust had parched her throat to such an extent that she found herself totally voiceless.

"Come along, now!" the man said impatiently. "I can't stand here all day, even if you can. What's your business?"

Elvira tried again, straining desperately at her vocal chords, but was still unable to summon up even a squeak. Then, quite without warning, she dissolved into tears.

"Here, here!" A look of panic replaced the impatience on the gateman's face. Wheeling round, he waved frantically with his one arm towards a lorry that was parked farther along the driveway in the shade of a building. "Miss Kindness!" he bellowed. "Can you come? Emergency!"

Immediately a grey-haired figure in trousers and a brown tunic jumped down from the driver's seat to come running across, as the man unlocked the gate.

"What on earth?" she was demanding as she bore down on them. Then, catching sight of Elvira, dishevelled, with tears coursing down her grimy cheeks, Miss Kindness exclaimed, "Oh, poor lamb!" and gathered her into an embrace that lasted until Elvira's stormy sobbing had abated.

"And now," she said gently, holding Elvira at arm's length, "who are you, poor, dusty little lady? And how can we help you?"

Elvira's outburst of weeping had restored her voice. "Please," she replied tremulously, "I want to see Mrs Rhoda Preston who works here. I'm her stepdaughter, Elvira, and they thought I should come because there's a letter arrived from France . . . only it's not in Dad's writing . . . so it might be . . . urgent."

She produced the letter from her pocket and held it out for inspection. The gatekeeper and Miss Kindness both nodded solemnly. After a moment Miss Kindness said decisively, "Best thing would be for me to take you to the women's rest-room, young Elvira. And I'll send someone off to find your stepmother. What do you think?"

Elvira nodded gratefully. All she wanted at that moment was to sit down indoors away from dust and petrol fumes and to will some strength back into her shaky legs.

"Come on, then!" Miss Kindness instructed her cheerfully, and they set off past the lorry and along a pathway between workshops whose doors lay wide open because of the heat. Elvira could see women wearing uniforms like Rhoda's and wielding noisy electric drills, hammering at pieces of wood or painting aeroplane wings. She was glad when they finally arrived at a wooden building which bore a notice saying, *Canteen and Rest Room*. But it was only when she was comfortably settled in a chair in a shady corner awaiting Rhoda's arrival that she suddenly realized that the worst part of her ordeal was still to come.

When Rhoda finally did appear she had already been told the reason for Elvira's visit. So with a brief little nod she held out her hand for the letter and swiftly slit it open with her thumbnail. Then she stood quite motionless, staring ahead of her. There was a minute of leaden silence before she turned to Miss Kindness who had withdrawn to a discreet distance.

"Please, miss," she said, in an odd, trembling voice that Elvira had never heard before, "I can't seem to be able to bring myself to look at it . . . so I wonder if you'd be good enough to read it out aloud for us."

"Of course," Miss Kindness said quietly, stepping forward to take the letter. "If you're sure that's what you want . . ."

"I'm sure," Rhoda replied, sitting down beside Elvira.

Miss Kindness gave a smothered little sigh, unfolded the single, thin blue sheet of paper, and began to read clearly and calmly.

"Beaussart, France. May the twenty-sixth, 1918
    Dear Mrs Preston,
            I thought I should write to you to let you know
about your husband, Tom. He has been missing since the
first or second of May. I can't tell the date exactly as I was
only told after we came out of the trenches, and no one
could remember when he was seen last. I'm sorry to have
to write and tell you this bad news, but I felt I had to
before you got the official word, Tom and me being such
good mates. Not that I've given up hope. Not by a long
way. And I'm sure you won't either.
            Tom's friend and yours,
                Bill Paton (Lance-Corporal)"

Elvira heard Rhoda give a single choked sob and Miss
Kindness's gentle voice say, "Oh, my dears!" Then she felt
suddenly very sick and icily cold, and at the same time a
ringing started up in her ears that grew louder and louder until
it filled her head and she slipped from the chair with a bump
into a velvety blackness.

9

The Angel

When Elvira opened her eyes it was to find herself lying flat on
her back on the wooden floor with Rhoda and Miss Kindness
kneeling on either side of her, each rubbing a wrist.

"She won't have had anything to eat," Rhoda was saying
fretfully.

"And the heat won't have helped," Miss Kindness remarked.
Elvira hadn't looked properly at Miss Kindness before. Now
she could see that she was a brown-skinned, leathery-looking
little woman with a pleasantly creased face.

"I'm all right now," Elvira assured them, but her voice was

treacherously shaky as she was gently helped into a sitting position.

"There!" said Rhoda with a show of cheerfulness. "Now you look more like our Elvie! Feeling better are you, love?"

Elvira nodded slowly. She felt strange, as though she'd been on a long and tiring journey. "Need I go back to school, Rhoda?" she faltered after a moment. "I don't feel much like it."

"Of course you needn't!" Rhoda assured her. Then she added, "But we'll have to get you back to Frissington to collect Artie from Mrs Boniface . . . How did you get here anyway, Elvie? I never thought to ask."

Elvira explained about Thomas Crow's motor-bicycle, and Rhoda looked glum. "Well, Thomas'll never think of calling back to see if you want to be taken home. That's for sure!" she sighed. "So I don't know what we're going to do about you."

"Perhaps I do, though!" Miss Kindness put in all at once. "I've to run over to the air-station this afternoon to collect a smashed plane. And I don't see why I shouldn't go via the Frissingtons. I'll just run along and check with the boss. Won't be a sec!"

"Nice, isn't she?" Rhoda remarked brightly, as she got to her feet and helped Elvira back into the chair. "A proper toff, they say. Lives in some big house in Ipswich with her father. Never had a job till she came here. But you should just see her drive that great lorry about, twisting and turning it! Better than any of the men she is!" Rhoda was talking so fast that she had become quite breathless. And her eyes were funny, Elvira thought. Black and hard and shiny like pieces of coal.

Miss Kindness evidently thought that Rhoda looked strange too. For when she came back to announce that she could indeed take Elvira in her lorry, she added gently, "There would be room for you too, Mrs Preston. Why not ask if you can have the rest of the day free? You're still suffering from shock. I can see it."

"No thank you, miss. I'm best working," Rhoda replied sharply, making for the door as though she were afraid of being forcibly detained. "Carry on as usual. That's what we'll have to do. That's what Tom would want. Thanks for taking Elvie, though!" And she vanished almost as she finished speaking.

Miss Kindness stared sadly at the closed door for a moment, then squared her shoulders and turned to Elvira. "Well, now!" she said cheerfully. "Do you feel fit enough to travel yet? Or would you like a bite to eat in the canteen before we leave?"

Elvira, feeling she couldn't cope with more strangers, said she would prefer to go straight home and Miss Kindness nodded understandingly. As they walked back towards the lorry in the scorching noonday sun she put a hand on Elvira's shoulder. "You mustn't give up hope, you know," she said firmly. "There's a good chance your father will turn up. I've heard of several missing men who have. And you must try to help your stepmother. This is going to be a great strain for her."

Elvira nodded because there was no point in doing anything else. She could hardly explain to Miss Kindness that now she felt even more detached from Rhoda than before. That Dad had been like an anchor holding them together. And that with him 'missing' Elvira already felt as alone in the world as Clarry Rae.

"Up we go, then, young lady!" Miss Kindness gave Elvira a helpful shove into the lorry's open front, then darted round to the other side to climb aboard herself. "She has an electric self-starter!" she informed Elvira proudly. Then added with a wry smile, "Mind you! That's her only redeeming feature. She's so bumpy it's unbelievable! I can't go above ten miles an hour along the country roads. And when the weather's cold my legs and feet turn to ice!" As she spoke the engine stuttered into life and the lorry moved towards the gate which the one-armed man held open for them. Then with some energetic pulling on the wheel, Miss Kindness turned the lumbering vehicle towards the left and they started sedately, if a trifle noisily, along the deserted main road.

"Where exactly in Frissington St Peter do you live?" Miss

Kindness enquired, after she had ascertained that Elvira was as comfortable as possible. When Elvira shouted into her ear that she was from Frissington Angel, the little woman jerked around so sharply that they almost ran into the ditch.

"You don't mean to say you're an 'angel'!" she exclaimed, straightening the lorry skilfully. "Why, that's wonderful!" Then, obviously aware of Elvira's puzzled eyes upon her, she added. "My dear old nanny was an 'angel', Elvira! And a very proud one! I was brought up on tales about that place."

Twenty yards ahead a tumbril loaded with hay, pulled out of a fieldgate and Miss Kindness braked to walking-pace with an impatient, "Tut".

"Has anyone found that lost angel yet, by the way?" she asked, smiling reminiscently. Turning she encountered a blank stare from Elvira. "You do know the story about Frissington's angel?" she added doubtfully.

"I knew there was some story about an angel in the church," Elvira replied, her brow wrinkling. "But I don't rightly know what."

"Oh, my dear!" The lorry stopped dead to allow the slow-moving cart to draw a little ahead. "It's a lovely story," Miss Kindness went on enthusiastically. "The angel was a real, gold angel — a cherub. Three feet high. Imagine it, Elvira! Plundered from the Armada by a local gentleman. To salve his conscience he gave it to the church — Frissington St Paul's church it was then. But the angel became so famous that the village soon became known as Frissington Angel."

"I didn't know that!" Elvira exclaimed, feeling suddenly interested and less depressed. "What happened to the angel, then? Did you say it was lost?"

"Indeed it was!" Miss Kindness replied, edging the lorry slowly forward again. "And my nanny, bless her, could remember when it happened. It was during the Napoleonic Wars. 1803 or 1804, maybe. People were afraid that the terrible Napoleon and his Frenchmen were going to invade England. So they started to hide their valuables. And the people of Frissington Angel hid their golden cherub — only, whatever

50

went wrong, no one could ever find him again."

"Do you think he was stolen?" Elvira asked, her brain fully alert now.

"Who knows?" Miss Kindness shrugged. "But, according to what Nanny said, Frissington Angel's luck went with him. The village never prospered after that. The big estate was broken up and the cottages sold to shopkeepers and tradesmen in the towns. And they wouldn't spend money on repairs or improvements. A lot of the farmers moved away. There was unemployment and riots and Frissington Angel just went slowly downhill, so to speak."

Elvira nodded. "It does look a bit sad today," she admitted reluctantly. "Dad says some of the cottages aren't fit for pigs. The Larters don't even have a proper stair, you know. Just a rickety ladder up to their bedrooms! And the ceilings not even six foot high! It isn't good enough!"

Miss Kindness turned briefly to smile at Elvira, an approving smile that showed she sympathized with the girl's indignation.

"You'll just have to find that lost angel, my dear," she told her, accelerating as the haywagon finally turned into a farmyard on the left. "Then Frissington Angel's luck might turn again. Imagine them all forgetting about it, though," she murmured, more to herself than to Elvira. "Whatever would Nanny have thought!"

At eight o'clock that evening Elvira was sitting on the old wooden bench at the back of Frissington Angel church. She had gone there on the pretext of picking more goosegrass. But in fact she had only wanted to escape from the cottage to which, since teatime, there had been a continuous procession of sympathetic friends and neighbours.

Rhoda had looked more normal when she arrived home, though her swollen face and red eyes showed that she had been weeping. She had sat down straight away to write a letter to Gran and Granfer Preston in Yorkshire and as she gave it to

51

Elvira to post, she announced that her supervisor had insisted she take the two weeks' leave due to her. "Artie'll enjoy that, anyway," she had sighed. "Not that old Mrs Boniface hasn't a heart of gold! But he hasn't the freedom there that he has at home."

It didn't seem to occur to Rhoda that it would be a treat for Elvira too, not having to rush home every day to fetch the water, cook the dinner and mind Arthur! I might as well not exist, she had thought bitterly, as she had hurried down to Frissington St Peter post office.

It had been the same story when Rhoda's friends and neighbours had started trooping in. Not one of them had thought to sympathize with Elvira about her dad. It was to Rhoda and little Arthur (blissfully unaware of the reason for all the stir) that they had offered their condolences and advice. Elvira had sat ignored in a corner until she had quietly asked Rhoda's permission to leave. Now she was feeling more lonely and wretched than she had felt in the whole of her life.

"Good evening, Elvira! May I join you?" The Reverend Robson-Turner's quiet voice broke into Elvira's reflections, making her jump. She looked up with an embarrassed little nod, surprised to find the rector here since Frissington Angel church had been closed for the duration of the War.

"Beautiful evening," the rector remarked with a sigh as he sat down. Then after a moment, he said, "Terribly sorry to hear about your father, Elvira. I'll be praying for his safe return."

Elvira thanked him. She had turned her head to the left and now found herself looking down on the backs of the row of cottages that ran up from Frissington Angel green towards the church. The tiny patches of garden at the back were little more than yards of hard-baked clay with their broken-down outhouses and communal earthclosets. The thatched roofs had bald patches. And Elvira could see at least one tiny side window three-quarters patched with brown paper and cardboard.

"Have you heard the story of the lost Frissington angel, sir?" she turned suddenly to ask the rector.

He nodded. "Only once, I think. An old lady who used to live in the Honeyballs' cottage told me about it."

"I'd never heard it! Not until today!" Elvira exclaimed petulantly, as though she felt she had been deliberately excluded from a village secret.

"No . . . I suppose the place has lost its traditions along with its heart," the Reverend Robson-Turner commented, more to himself than to Elvira. Then he turned to her to say, "Families don't remain here for generations as they do in some villages, Elvira. It's become a kind of temporary stopping place. People arrive and then they move on in a few years. So they don't know the old stories. They . . ." He stopped suddenly, head on one side, and then put his finger to his lips. Someone inside the church had started to play the organ very softly. The sound — like fairy bells, Elvira thought — floated out to hang on the still, evening air.

"Who is it?" she whispered curiously to the rector. As far as Elvira knew, there hadn't been an organist in the Frissingtons since Miss Allison had left.

"One of the German prisoners," the Reverend Robson-Turner whispered back. "I've promised to bring him up here when I can, poor lad!"

Little icicles of apprehension jabbed at Elvira's spine. She would have taken a hasty leave of the rector had the music not held her there. For now, beneath the fairy bells it was as though a golden voice were singing. And although Elvira knew that it was the organ's voice, she couldn't help closing her eyes and imagining that she was listening to the golden angel sing.

When the enchanting music finally died away, the rector said quietly, "That piece was called *Jesu, Joy of Man's Desiring*, Elvira. It was composed by a German musician called Bach. And you won't often hear it played as superbly as that."

Elvira nodded, still a little dreamy. Then with an abrupt "Good night, sir!" to the rector, she rose and ran off round the side of the church and down to the gate. It had suddenly struck her that the German might come out of the church to speak to

53

the Reverend Robson-Turner and she didn't want to be there when that happened!

And yet it was funny, Elvira reflected, as she sauntered back down towards the green. For just a short while ago she had been feeling quite dreadful – wretched and lonely, not knowing whether she would ever see Dad again. And that was the fault of those hateful Germans! But now, because of that music she'd been listening to, she felt much better. Stronger and much more hopeful. And that was because of Germans, too! The one who had composed the music. And the prisoner who'd been playing it.

Elvira arrived home just as Mrs Diaper was leaving. When she saw Rhoda's white, drawn face she felt a pang of remorse. "You look wholly drained, Rhoda!" she exclaimed. "Why don't you get up to bed and I'll bring you some cocoa?"

"No point in that," Rhoda sighed. "I'd just toss and turn. I think I'll sit out at the back and do some mending till the light goes." She was about to walk through to the scullery when she suddenly stopped and turned round. "Thanks for the thought, though," she added. "That was real considerate of you."

" 'S all right," Elvira replied casually. But for the first time in ages she and her stepmother exchanged a companionable smile.

10
Changes

After she had heard the organ music, it seemed to Elvira that the whole pattern of her life began to change. For one thing she was on better terms with Rhoda than she had been for a long time. And at school Mr Christmas was less caustic. There were other changes too. Since Rhoda was at home and unable to shop in Ipswich she had been forced to register again with Mrs Fisher for her rationed goods. This humiliation was only made tolerable for her by the shopkeeper's surprisingly forgiving attitude.

Then on Thursday, the sixth of June, it looked as though the weather too were going to change at last. Elvira awoke to find the bedroom she shared with Arthur not bright with hard, yellow sunshine as it had been every morning for weeks, but bathed in a subdued, pearly-grey light. Outside, beneath an overcast sky, it was decidedly cool with a little breeze that chased around the playground setting everyone shivering.

" 'S going to rain," Clarry promised Elvira. "You won't have to cart those old water-buckets much longer, Elvie!"

Mr Turpin, a Frissington St Peter farmer who was also a school manager, evidently thought likewise. For he came bustling into school just before morning break to ask whether some older pupils could be spared to help rake up his hay that had been cut the previous afternoon. "They promised me a squad of them Land Girls, but they haven't showed up!" he explained to Mr Christmas in some exasperation.

Mr Christmas was quite happy to part with Standard 6 for the remainder of the morning so the farmer led them smartly across the playground and along the road to his hayfield.

"Think he'll pay us?" Ethel Foster asked, trotting breathlessly along beside Elvira.

" 'Course he will!" Lizzie Pitt called over her shoulder. "Else there'd be trouble with our folks. Wouldn't there, Elvie?"

" 'Spect so," Elvira agreed. It hadn't occurred to her that they would probably receive some small payment for their work. But now the thought cheered her up. Because with Arthur's birthday only two days off and his present still to be bought, even a farthing would be a welcome addition to her thin purse.

Indeed, as Elvira energetically wielded the heavy, old rake that the farmer had handed her and felt the cool breeze tickle the nape of her neck, she would have been quite satisfied with her lot, had it not been for the fact that Clarry was at her elbow, bursting to talk about the Sanctuary! Already he had smuggled a bucket and shovel up there. He had told Elvira so earlier that morning. And she knew that he had been making plans about the garden. All of which caused her to feel more and more uncomfortable as she raked fiercely at the strewn hay, and tried to ignore the boy's excited whisperings. For the truth was that, during the past few days, Elvira had begun to see her place as being beside Rhoda. It was as though a new, sisterly feeling had sprung up between them, as though the Sanctuary belonged in another world.

But how to explain this to Clarry with his eyes shining in that peaky face of his? In her desperation Elvira avoided the issue by turning to old Grandpa Larter who was raking wheezily on her left.

"Ever hear about the Frissington angel? The one that got lost, Grandpa?" she asked hastily, clutching at the first wisp of an idea that came floating into her head.

The old man turned to look at her from beneath bristling brows. " 'Course I have!" he replied. "Caused all our troubles that, didn't it? Leastways so my old dad used to say. Nothing never flourishes near Frissington Angel. Brickworks. Silk factory. They all shut up in the end. Reckon there's a curse on the place, true enough."

"What's he on about?" Clarry whispered in Elvira's right ear.

"Nothing much. Curses and things," Elvira replied shortly, moving forward to start work in a new line of rakers.

In the end the schoolchildren were each given a penny for their morning's labours, and when they trooped out of school that afternoon they could see the hay already being carted from the field to the safety of the rickyard. The sky was pewter-coloured now, but not a drop of rain had fallen. Elvira, hurrying on ahead to avoid Clarry, raced to Mrs Fisher's shop for Arthur's birthday present. The shop door was closed when she reached it and its green blind pulled down, so that when she pushed it open she was taken aback to find at least a dozen customers crammed inside and Police Constable Appleby stationed on Mrs Fisher's side of the counter.

"Won't keep you a moment, dear. Don't run away!" Mrs Fisher exhorted Elvira, pinning her against the door with a sharp, black eye.

"And who else thinks they saw this motorcar, now?" the constable was asking, leaning over the counter, pencil poised above notebook.

"I did," a thin woman called Mrs Groom, piped up. "Great grey motor that was! Creeping up the hill, silent as a ghost!"

"And did you see it stop, my dear?" the policeman asked, writing busily.

"Reckon it must have done!" Mrs Groom's bulbous eyes were almost popping out. " 'Cos suddenly there were these two lights shooting up in the sky! That was signalling with its headlights, you see!"

"And right outside the factory gates! Wasn't it, Emmy?" Mrs Fisher put in meaningfully.

"That it was!" Mrs Groom confirmed.

"And Grandpa says they're bringing fifty more prisoners here next month to help with the harvest!" a familiarly penetrating voice sang out from the rear of the shop as Sophie Christmas hoisted herself up on a stool.

"Saints above! We'll all be murdered in our beds!" Mrs Fisher wailed.

"Oh, I wouldn't say that!" Constable Appleby remarked calmly. "Mind you, it wouldn't do no harm if you was all to keep your eyes and ears open," he added after a moment. "Watch out for strangers. Or unusual flashing lights. Things like that."

Elvira didn't wait to hear any more. It scared her to listen to all those sensible adults talk so fearfully about spies and murder. She hurried home to report to Rhoda, hoping to be laughingly reassured. But it seemed that Rhoda too was beginning to take the 'Frissington spy' stories seriously.

"Fares like old Mrs Boniface saw something the other night too, Elvie," she burst out. "Lights up on the church tower, she said. It was around two o'clock in the morning and she'd got up to sit by the window because of the heat."

"But why here?" Elvira demanded, her voice squeaky with alarm.

"Mrs Fisher reckons it's all to do with those prisoners," Rhoda informed Elvira. "There might be some really important Hun amongst that lot. Someone they want back right now to help them win the War."

"But all the important prisoners are in Donnington Hall in Leicestershire!" Elvira protested. "Dad said so."

"But this one would be in disguise of course. Just looking like an ordinary soldier," Rhoda retorted. Then she added unhappily, "There's always the chance they're after the aeroplane-workers. A few bombs on the Frissingtons, a break-out from the Camp and where would we all be?"

"Did Mrs Fisher say that too?" Elvira enquired, looking out of the front window at the grey sky.

Rhoda nodded. "She wants those prisoners moved," she declared, "before it's too late."

Elvira had a chance to inspect Mrs Fisher furtively the following afternoon when she called in to buy Arthur's present. While Elvira picked through a box of odd twopenny toys, Mrs Fisher retired to her seat in the corner to drink her tea. She was a comparative newcomer to Frissington St Peter, having arrived in 1914 when Mr Dykes, the shop's former owner, had sold up and gone into the army. She was a large woman with a doughy face, raven black hair and tiny, sharp, black eyes. To begin with the locals had tended to find fault with her and had regretted Mr Dykes' departure. But after the story had gone round that Mrs Fisher was a poor, childless, widow woman trying to start up in business with a small inheritance, her customers had become more tolerant. She had been accepted in the end and indeed lately she had become quite a force in the Frissingtons with her war-work and her unrelenting campaign against the prisoner-of-war camp. Not that Elvira liked her much. Not even now, when Mrs Fisher insisted on pressing two bright tin soldiers into her hand for the price of one.

"You take them, my dear!" she said, her fat chins wobbling

with emotion. "You're a soldier's daughter. You deserve that little bit extra!"

And tomorrow she'll be hiding in the doorway, hoping to catch me running over her white step, Elvira reflected as she left. "She's a funny one and no mistake!"

Nevertheless she was glad to have the two soldiers to give to Arthur. He loved his little 'army' and would spend hours marching them around the rug. As she hurried up the dusty hill beneath another heavy sky, Elvira decided she would play with her little brother after his birthday tea. She could make up a story about a battle, and Arthur could act it out with his soldiers. He loved anything like that. And since it was a little celebration, Rhoda might even join in too.

11

Two's Company

As soon as Elvira walked into the living-room that evening, Rhoda nodded grim-faced towards a sheet of paper that was propped up against the clock on the mantleshelf. It was a letter from the military authorities in France beginning, "We regret to inform you that 305 Private Thomas Preston, H. Company, 4th Battalion Anglian Regiment, has gone missing in action."

"Well, it doesn't tell us anything we don't know," Elvira remarked reasonably, and turned to find Rhoda glaring at her with hurt, angry eyes.

Thinking to smooth matters over she fished in her skirt pocket and produced the two soldiers for a delighted Arthur to place in the little wheelbarrow that his mother had given him for his birthday. "Thought I might play with him after his birthday tea," she informed Rhoda.

"Oh . . . we've had that," Rhoda said casually. "Wasn't hardly enough for two, Elvie, far less three! A little bit of jelly and a spot of custard and a tiny chocolate cake with a candle on it. That's all I could manage. There's some nice broth for you,

59

though. And some cold rice-pudding, if you'd like it."

"Thanks," Elvira mumbled, fighting against the lump that had formed in her throat. It was the feeling of once again being excluded that hurt so much. A couple of crumbs from Arthur's cake would have satisfied her that she was part of his birthday celebration. Surely Rhoda ought to have realized that!

There was yet another blow after Elvira had finished her solitary meal.

"You can run off now, Elvie," Rhoda announced. "Have an evening to yourself for once. I'm going to leave the chores till morning so's I can play with Artie till his bedtime. Aren't I, my man?" Arthur, sitting on his mother's knee, looked up at her adoringly. Elvira slipped away through the scullery without a word.

"You-fool-you-fooool-you-fooool!" a wood-pigeon trilled from the fir-trees behind Mrs Boniface's as Elvira stamped by along the Frissington St Peter road. Yes! That was true enough, she thought bitterly! She was a fool. A fool for ever having thought that she and Rhoda could become close because Dad had gone missing! She wasn't needed at home. Not wanted, even! Rhoda and Arthur were perfectly happy on their own. Her quick, angry strides carried her up the goose-grass path and through the coppice, almost before she had realized it. Only when she stood before the Sanctuary itself did she finally simmer down and begin to feel quietly remorseful. On this sunless evening the house looked bleak and neglected. How could she have betrayed it so, she wondered ruefully! How could she ever have thought of letting Clarry down!

Pushing her way into the hall Elvira almost fell over the handle of a broom. Beside it was a shovel and a bucket, and, propped against the wall a mop, a feather duster and a garden spade. Elvira's remorse grew as she looked at the collection. Then she suddenly swooped on the broom and the shovel and carried them into the room on the left. Our lilac parlour, she thought fondly as she closed her eyes and sniffed. Must have been a treat to sit in here when it was all spick and span and furnished. Then, as though a spring had been released inside her she moved into action, down on her knees beneath the back window, scraping and sweeping. She worked on the floor for two hours or more using the edge of the shovel to scrape up mildew and hard-caked layers of dirt, as well as the droppings of generations of birds and mice. She created blizzards of blinding, stifling dust with the broom. At the end of it all she felt damp and limp with beads of perspiration rolling like tears down her flushed face. But the brown, tiled floor was visible in its entirety now, needing only a wash and a polish to bring the bloom black to its surface. It was a start, Elvira thought. Her dream was beginning to take shape.

She tiptoed out into the grey evening as though afraid of awaking some invisible sleeper inside, and made her way back to Rhoda and Arthur feeling tranquil and content.

"Well, I didn't do it! So there!"

"Who did, then, if it wasn't you, Clarry Rae?"

"How do I know? . . . But it's not the only funny thing that's happened here. I'll tell you that!"

Elvira and Clarry glared at each other the following Sunday afternoon across the length of the lilac parlour. Between them Elvira's floor, upon which she had expended so much effort, was strewn with withered grass-cuttings.

"Couldn't have been a bird, could it?" Clarry asked at last, sitting down with a bump beneath the window.

"Well, if it was — and if this is its nest — it must be a whopping monster!" Elvira declared, and almost immediately was overcome by a fit of giggles. Clarry joined in, and their laughter set them back on good terms.

"But if it wasn't you . . ." Elvira went on.

"And it wasn't!" Clarry said firmly.

"It's just as though someone had walked through a hayfield and then come in here," Elvira said, frowning. "And yet nothing's been touched. None of the cleaning things you brought up, Clarry. I can't believe anyone else knows about this place."

"Well, if you ask me — I think it's ghosts!" Clarry volunteered suddenly. His voice was almost a shout and his face had turned pink and was screwed up with embarrassment.

"What d'you say that for?" Elvira queried, looking at her friend in alarm.

"Well . . . I smelled this cigarette smoke, see. Twice when I came up here evenings. And the second time I heard like a piano playing . . . just before I got to the door. Just as though there'd been folks sitting in here, Elvie, smoking and having a party. I've been trying to tell you for days!" he finished accusingly. "But you'd never stop and listen."

"You mean the Sanctuary's haunted, Clarry?" Elvira felt her scalp tingle, but not unpleasantly as she whispered the words.

"What else can it be?" Clarry asked unhappily. "I didn't imagine it, I swear, Elvie! I'm not that sort of person."

Elvira sat down cross-legged on the floor and stared into space. Finally she said, "But you don't feel the house is unfriendly, Clarry, do you?"

The boy shook his head. Elvira gave a sigh of relief. "No," she declared firmly. "Nor do I. Just the opposite in fact. So even if there are ghosts, and I'm not saying I believe that, then it needn't alter our plans. Because if they minded us being here we'd know it. Don't you think so?"

Clarry nodded, but not positively enough to satisfy Elvira.

"You're not scared, are you?" she enquired anxiously.

"Scared! Who's scared?" Clarry's face burned with indignation.

"That's all right, then," Elvira said appeasingly. "I just wondered." She jumped to her feet. "Let's go and look at that old well," she suggested. "That well's what my dad would call 'our main asset', Clarry! Specially during a drought like this."

The well was to prove a disappointment though. For, having hacked with the spade at the encircling nettles and thistles, and pulled up knee-high grass and buttercups by the armful, it was only to find the well sealed with a plug of concrete.

"Can't move it!" Clarry groaned, abandoning his efforts to

lever it up with the spade. "Here! Elvie!" he went on with an expression of alarm. "You don't think there's a . . ."

"No! I don't think there's a body in it!" Elvira interrupted testily. "That's been done to stop one falling in most likely. Means we'll have to fetch our water from the old pump though till we can get that blessed thing opened up."

"Never mind!" Clarry consoled her. "There's a hundred things we can be getting on with, Elvie. Things like building a woodpile. And making a hen-run. Want to see my plan of campaign?"

He strode back to sit on the doorstep, drawing a sheet of paper from his fraying trouser pocket, and handed it proudly to Elvira. She sat down beside him, and as they bent over the paper, their shadows fused imperceptibly into one.

12
Star of Hope

The promise of rain had been a false one even though the sun sulked constantly now behind a grey curtain of cloud. Beans yellowed and shrank in the cottage gardens, and peas that ought to have been plumping out were still wafer thin. The drought too was responsible for the plague of caterpillars that were stripping bare all the oak trees in the neighbourhood.

"The butcher called this morning and he's heard it's that monster German gun, the one they call 'Big Bertha', that's interfering with the clouds and holding the rain back," Rhoda told Elvira the following Tuesday evening.

"Mr Christmas says that if they fired Big Bertha in our school yard, it would kill people in London," Elvira remarked pensively.

Rhoda digested this piece of information silently while cutting the crust from Arthur's bread. Then she suddenly burst out, "Oh! I do wish something nice would happen!

63

Anything! Anywhere! There's nothing but bad news nowadays, Elvie! The Huns nearly at Paris. Food getting scarcer. Spies creeping about. No one smiles any more. Hadn't you noticed?"

The Reverend Robson-Turner, however, was smiling quite radiantly when he came striding into Mr Christmas's classroom on the morning of the twelfth of June. "Have they heard?" he enquired of the headmaster excitedly. "Have you told them about the great discovery?"

"I was just about to as a matter of fact," Mr Christmas replied testily. "But since you've obviously come along specially, Rector . . ."

"Thank you so much!" The rector's beam encompassed both the disconsolate headmaster and his wide-eyed, attentive pupils.

They've found the angel, Elvira thought immediately. They must have! She had been thinking about the golden angel and its possible whereabouts just before the rector had appeared and now her heart began to bump excitedly against her ribs.

But when the Reverend Robson-Turner said in a softer tone, "Children! Something most wonderful has happened. A new star has appeared in the sky," then Elvira's excitement faded. After all, there were so many stars in the sky; what did another one matter? Gradually, however, she began to be caught up by the rector's joyous enthusiasm. For one thing, it seemed that the new star had local connections, having been first spotted by a Suffolk lady who had telephoned the news from Stowmarket to the Royal Observatory. Moreover the star was to be found in that part of the heavens called the Milky Way, a name which had always conjured up in Elvira's mind a delightful vision of a shining, white, marble highroad.

"The star is to be called Nova Aquilae," the rector told them. "And I like to believe this is a star of hope. A sign of good cheer especially sent to us to help us through these dark, difficult days." His kindly eyes met Elvira's for a moment. Then he went on, "The most wonderful thing is that Nova Aquilae is the result of a fiery collision between two other worlds thousands and thousands of years ago. And it has taken all this time for the light caused by that accident to travel through space to us."

Sophie Christmas cornered Elvira and Clarry in the playground at lunchtime just as they were about to start discussing their plans for the Sanctuary. "Do you believe all that? About how that new star came into the sky?" she asked them, her eyes narrowed unpleasantly.

" 'Course we believe it!" Clarry exclaimed. "The old rector's hardly going to stand up and tell us a pack of lies now, is he?"

Sophie shrugged, and her sharp little face took on a vindictive expression. "All I know about our rector is that he's a very good friend to the German prisoners in the Factory!" she declared. "A very good friend indeed! You ask Mrs Fisher if you don't believe me!"

"Mrs Fisher! Mrs Fisher!" Elvira's cheeks flamed. "That woman ought to get a cage to set you in, Sophie Christmas! 'Cos you're nothing but her little parrot," she called over her shoulder as she hauled Clarry off to a more private spot.

Elvira and Clarry decided to go up to the Sanctuary that evening. "Old Flintstones won't miss me," the boy assured Elvira. "After the nippers are in bed she gets her head stuck in some slushy love story and she doesn't know what's going on. Doesn't care either."

Elvira's evenings were free this week too because Rhoda was still on leave from the factory and didn't need help with the chores. The only injunction Elvira had from her stepmother was that she mustn't wander far from the village because of the spy. "If he exists, that is!" Rhoda had added with an unconvincing little laugh.

So Elvira made a start on cleaning the Sanctuary's kitchen floor, while Clarry inspected the stables and outhouses, appearing triumphantly at intervals with pieces of old timber for his woodpile in the back yard.

"Might be able to come up on Saturday night too," he informed Elvira breathlessly as he dumped his last armful of wood before they set off for home. "Can't do much on the allotments now till we get some rain."

"Rain? What's that?" Elvira groaned, looking up at the colourless sky. "I can't even remember what it feels like, Clarry!"

"I can!" retorted Clarry grimly, looking down at his old boots. It suddenly struck Elvira that poor Clarry, who became a prisoner whenever it rained heavily, must be the only person in the Frissingtons who was dreading the end of the drought.

"I'll bring some scones and milk if we come on Saturday," she promised him, and watched with satisfaction as the brightness returned to his face.

But as it happened there was to be no work done at the Sanctuary on Saturday. For when Elvira arrived back at the cottage, it was to find Rhoda sitting awaiting her with an open letter on her lap. And so excited was she that she even failed to notice the state of Elvira's pinafore, coated as it was with grime from the Sanctuary kitchen.

"Mrs Johnson that sits beside me on the factory truck, brought this along when you were out, Elvira," Rhoda announced. "It's from that Miss Kindness that brought you home in her lorry. She asked Mrs Johnson if she could deliver it for her. It's an invitation for you, my gel!"

"For me? From Miss Kindness?" Elvira exclaimed disbelievingly. "Are you sure?"

" 'Course I'm sure!" Rhoda laughed. "Think I can't read! She wants to come over in her car and take you back to her house next Saturday at two. Says you can take a friend with you and all. Here! See for yourself."

Elvira took the white sheet of paper in a hand that trembled so much that the words fairly danced before her eyes.

"Cor! Rhoda! Look at this!" she breathed at last. "She says we might go on the river in a boat!"

Rhoda nodded. "That Miss Kindness! She's a rum 'un and no mistake!" she commented. "I told Mrs Johnson to thank her and to say you'll be pleased to accept. All right?"

"Oh, yes!" Elvira replied, her face alight. "Can I take Clarry

Rae with me, Rhoda? He'd love it! I know he would."

"What? That poor, little old scarecrow?" Rhoda looked doubtful for a moment, then nodded her head. "Well, why not if it's all right with the Flint woman? He'll have few enough treats in that place, poor lad, if it's anything like the kids' home I was reared in."

It was nine o'clock on Friday morning before a jubilant Clarry could assure Elvira that he had Miss Flint's reluctant permission to go on the Saturday outing. "Reckon she just couldn't think of a reason for me not to go though she tried hard enough." He grinned as they hurried through the school gates. And as the urgent clamour of Mr Christmas's handbell suddenly ceased, the boy added, "Looks like the rector was right about that star, Elvie. Things are brightening up for us already, aren't they?"

"M-m-m. Let's hope so," Elvira sighed. Then, seeing the school door begin to close, she grabbed Clarry's arm and they set off at a gallop across the deserted yard.

13

The Outing

On Saturday morning the sun returned unexpectedly to bake the cracked earth even harder. The old straw hat was put back on the head of Mitchells' donkey, morosely grazing the parched green.

"A perfect day for a drive!" Miss Kindness declared gaily as Elvira and Clarry clambered into the back of her gleaming little Ford. They rolled regally away from the Prestons' gate to a flutter of waving hands. For Rhoda and Arthur, the Honeyballs and old Mrs Boniface had all come out to give them a proper send-off. Then, as they wound their way through Frissington St Peter, they passed Sophie Christmas skipping in front of the schoolhouse and watched her jaw drop in amazement.

"There now! That'll give her something to chew on with her friend, Mrs Fisher!" Elvira remarked to Clarry with satisfaction.

But Clarry had no time for conversation. Scrubbed and polished, and looking as neat as was possible in his shabby clothes he was sitting ramrod-straight with his head swivelling from side to side so that he could drink in every detail of the passing scene. In several fields clover was still being carted. And once, a boy sitting on a load of hay looked down enviously on them over a hedge. It was, however, the passing traffic that held most interest for Elvira and Clarry. For, in addition to the market-goers in motors, on bicycles and in horse-drawn traps, there were army lorries, ambulances, trucks crammed with Land Girls, and occasionally troops of marching Boy Scouts.

"A little more comfortable than our last journey together, Elvira!" Miss Kindness bawled over her shoulder, as they sped along a quiet stretch of road at a breathtaking thirty miles per hour. Elvira's spirits flagged a little for the memory of the lorry ride had reminded her of her dad, and the fact that they had still heard no news of him. The worry gnawed away inside her like a toothache until the car suddenly slowed, turned left into a leafy lane, crossed a narrow bridge, then drew to a gentle halt on a grassy riverbank.

"Cor! Look! Look at that, Elvie!" Clarry leapt to his feet to point excitedly at the lively scene on the stretch of river ahead of them. Boys and young men were swimming from bank to bank or paddling in the shallows, while an assortment of little boats floated back and forth as their high-spirited occupants shouted, sang or shrieked with laughter.

"Oh, dear!" Miss Kindness exclaimed as she led the way down to a large boathouse, "I hadn't expected it to be quite so busy!" Then, as she turned to find her companions looking crest-fallen, she added hastily, "But never mind! We can battle our way through that lot and go on upstream where it's quieter. I'll just pop into the office and see if they have a free boat."

Ten minutes later, by dint of Miss Kindness's strenuous pulling on the oars, they were in another, more tranquil world. An enchanted world, Elvira felt, as the soft tresses of the bowing willows brushed across the top of her hand, trailing her fingers through the silky coolness of the green water. As they rounded a bend into yet another deserted stretch, Miss Kindness changed places with Clarry so that he might have a chance to 'wield the oars', as she put it.

"Never done it before, miss. But I'll have a go," he announced gamely, and flailed wildly for the first few strokes before he mastered the rhythm of the operation. Miss Kindness murmured a polite, "Well done!" but Elvira could see that she was staring very hard at Clarry's bony wrists, and finally she said quietly, "Clarry, dear. I'm just wondering . . . do you always have enough to eat where you live?"

"No, he does not!" Elvira put in fiercely. "He never has enough, Miss Kindness! A stale bun for his dinner and some watery soup for his supper! You're always hungry, Clarry. Aren't you, now?"

"Well . . . mostly," Clarry admitted, his happy grin fading only slightly. "Old Flintstones can't seem to manage the rations somehow. Always running out of food, she is."

"I see." Miss Kindness's sun-browned face became even more creased, as she stared thoughtfully at the far riverbank.

It was three-thirty when they finally returned to the boat-house, by which time both Elvira and Clarry were competent, if not expert, rowers. And fifteen minutes later, having honked their way masterfully through the hubbub of Ipswich, they turned in through a wide gateway and came to a halt before an imposing, decoratively-timbered brick house.

"It's got stained-glass windows like a church!" Elvira couldn't help exclaiming, as she dropped down on to the gravel driveway.

"Yes," Miss Kindness laughed. "Those are the hall windows. And when my three sisters and I were small, we would sit on the landing and pretend that we were in church, Elvira. It was a wonderful house for 'pretending' games."

"Do your sisters still live here?" Elvira asked, wondering how many strangers they would have to brave.

But Miss Kindness shook her head. "Dear me, no! They're all married and gone," she smiled. "There's just my father and myself here now. And Molly, our housekeeper. We rattle about like peas in a pod, but we love the old place so much we can't bear the idea of moving."

As she spoke she led them over to a little porch on the left side of which was the enormous oak front door. "In you go, children! Make yourselves at home!" she exhorted them, pushing the door open, and then calling out, "Father! Molly! We're here! Kettle on, please!"

Elvira caught her breath as she stepped into the spacious hall, with its tall windows sparkling red and gold in the afternoon sun, its grand staircase and great expanse of polished floor. Their hostess led them along to the right past two closed doors to which she pointed saying, "Library . . . drawing-room." A third door faced them at the back of the hall and Miss Kindness opened this quietly. Then with a chuckle and a shake of her head she exclaimed, "Yes! Just as I thought! Come in you two and meet the Sleeping Beauty."

An old gentleman was snoring gently in a chair by the open French window of a room which once more left Elvira speechless and wide-eyed. Clarry too gave a little gasp of admiration, but when Elvira turned to look at him she saw that his eyes were fixed on the round table in the centre of the room which was laden with plates of sandwiches, jellies, custards and cake.

"Come along, Father!" Miss Kindness called, walking over and gently shaking the old gentleman's shoulder. "Our visitors are here." And almost instantly Mr Kindness's bright eyes shot wide open and a surprisingly boyish smile spread over his face.

"Well! This is nice!" he exclaimed, springing to his feet, and coming over to pump his guests' hands energetically. "Clarry and Elvira. Clarry and Elvira!" he repeated, echoing his daughter's introduction. "Most kind of you to come. Like to see young faces about the place. Grandchildren all out in

70

America or Australia. We don't have much company nowadays."

"Can't afford to, sir. Not with the War and the rationing," a plump, aproned lady announced as she bustled in with a steaming teapot. "Took me all my time to rustle this lot up, I can tell you! Just lucky my brother killed an old hen this week else we wouldn't have had any sandwiches."

"I know, Molly. You're a marvel!" Miss Kindness declared gratefully. "I don't know how we'd manage without you."

"Nor do I," the housekeeper retorted smartly. Then as she turned to leave, her eyes fell on Clarry. "And you eat up, my lad," she admonished him. "Fares like you need to! Good gracious me! You're naught but skin and bone!"

Clarry needed no urging to do justice to the excellent tea. He ate seriously and silently, pausing occasionally to flash Miss Kindness or her father one of his bright, appreciative grins.

"Never enjoyed a tea like that! Ever!" he commented finally, sitting back replete and exhausted.

For Elvira, the best of the afternoon was still to come. For, when Miss Kindness said they might go and play anywhere in the house, she immediately asked if she could see the library.

"We'll go together," Miss Kindness told her, "because I'm a bookworm, too. And I'll probably be able to find a pile to take home with you."

"And you and I will go upstairs to the attics and find something more exciting to do," Mr Kindness told Clarry, putting his arm round the boy's shoulders and leading him to the door.

"You've never seen such a place!" Clarry whispered to Elvira later, as they rode home in the pearly light of the summer evening. "It's like a treasure-house, Elvie! There's a great rocking-horse, and a toy theatre, and masses of clockwork toys and musical boxes. Mr Kindness kept wanting to give me things to take back with me like his old stamp album. But it wouldn't have been any good. Old Flintstones would have confiscated it. I told him so."

"The library's like a treasure-house too," Elvira murmured, her arms clasped round the pile of books Miss Kindness had given her. Some of the titles she could remember without looking: *Christie's Old Organ*, *Alone in London*, *A Peep behind the Scenes*. Then there were some by Charles Dickens and Sir Walter Scott.

Clarry nudged her. "It's been the best day out I've ever had!" he exclaimed. "I'll never forget it! Will you, Elvie?"

"No." Elvira smiled sleepily, feeling her eyelids drooping.

But as the little Ford jogged on towards the Frissingtons, with Miss Kindness humming contentedly at the wheel, neither of its passengers could have guessed how this Saturday outing was to change the course of the summer ahead — and in Clarry's case, to transform his entire future.

14

Thunderclouds

"Can't say I feel like going back to that old factory! Not on a sunny day like this," Rhoda remarked to Elvira over their seven o'clock breakfast on Monday morning.

"Arthur'll miss you," Elvira sighed, already thinking of her afternoon's chores. "Shouldn't be surprised if he plays up today."

As it turned out though, Elvira had just deposited Arthur with Mrs Boniface and was making her way down Factory Hill when to her astonishment she saw Rhoda striding uphill towards her.

"All that journey for nothing!" Rhoda exclaimed angrily as they met. "We'd hardly picked up our tools before we were told to lay them down again. There's a strike on!"

"A strike! Of aeroplane workers!" Elvira gasped, wide-eyed. "But won't that help the Germans, Rhoda?"

"Us girls think so!" Rhoda replied tartly as she moved off.

"But you can't talk sense to those men. You'd really think some of them were fighting on the other side."

Elvira's mouth felt dry as she hurried on downhill. For hadn't Miss Kindness been saying only on Saturday how important the factory's aeroplanes were in defending England against German bombs? Surely there was something sinister about it all! Spies in the Frissingtons. A strike in the factory. She could feel the gooseflesh on her arms, despite the warm sun that was soaking through the long sleeves of her blouse.

"Coo-ee!" A piercing call from the other side of the road sent Elvira's heart leaping into her mouth. She looked round to find Mrs Fisher bearing down on her brandishing a roll of red and white paper.

"Take this down to the headmaster, dear!" she told Elvira peremptorily. "And be very careful with it. It's the notice about our Alexandra Day fête on Wednesday. For the Wounded Soldiers' Fund, you know. Did you remember about it?"

"Yes," Elvira replied, taking the paper. "We're having an afternoon holiday from school."

"Oh, yes! So you are. I was forgetting." The shopkeeper beamed. "Oh, that Mr Christmas is a fine man!" she continued. "Does everything he can to help our boys at the Front. Not like some that are more concerned about those German monsters from the Camp!"

"If you're talking about the rector, Mrs Fisher, then that just isn't true!" Elvira retorted, her cheeks aflame. And with a steely glare for the scowling woman she ran angrily over the crossroads and into School Lane. Honestly! she fumed inwardly. Who on earth did that Fisher woman think she was criticizing the rector like that, when a kinder, more generous gentleman would be hard to find? If it wasn't for the fact that her old fête was to help the wounded soldiers, she could almost have wished it to be a terrible flop.

As it turned out, the Alexandra Day fête was never to take place. For on Wednesday the long-awaited rain decided to arrive in style. It was just after five o'clock that morning when the first volley of thunder exploded above the Frissingtons, bouncing people out of their beds to bang windows down or pull them shut against a livid sky, across which danced jagged forks of lightning. The second crash wakened Arthur who stood up in his cot and began to wail. Elvira, lying comfortably in bed enjoying the storm, merely called, "There now. What you going on about? It's only an old thunderstorm, Artie!"

Almost instantly the door shot open and Rhoda flew in, her curly hair frizzed into a halo from being pressed against her pillow. "Well! That's nice!" she snapped, as she lifted Arthur into her arms. "Watching the poor little lamb yell his head off before you'll get up to see to him."

"He hadn't hardly opened his mouth," Elvira protested as a deafening cascade of thunder made the cottage shake and the room was illuminated with a succession of lightning flashes. "Cor!" she added involuntarily. "This must be exactly like it is in the Front Line trenches in France."

"What a thing to come out with," Rhoda gasped, her dark eyes glistening. "And your dad out there! You're so insensitive sometimes, Elvira Preston, it's hard to believe." And she stormed out with the whimpering Arthur.

"Thank goodness for that. Nice to have some peace and quiet," Elvira muttered, pulling a face after the pair. Takes everything out on me. Don't know what she'll do when I'm gone, she reflected sourly as she rolled on to her back to hear the rain better. It was really hissing down outside now, making it sound as though Mr Diaper were plunging a thousand red-hot irons into the cooling-trough in his forge.

It rained without stopping all morning. Sometimes in short-lived thundery downpours, but mostly with a steady, monotonous drumming that was audible in the classroom even above Mr Christmas's stentorian tones. Because it was Alexandra Day (so called after the king's mother) they had been asked to come to school wearing a rose in her memory. Elvira, who was fortunate in having a real waterproof coat that Rhoda had bought at a jumble-sale, had managed to preserve her red rose beneath it. But most of the others had arrived with little more than sodden balls of petals. Nevertheless they all stood up to sing enthusiastically,

> "Roses red and roses white
> Have blossomed the whole world o'er.
> But the sweetest Rose, old England knows,
> Was gathered on Denmark's shore."

They were just resuming their seats, when the classroom door burst open to admit a radiant-looking Clarry. The shining new boots he was wearing creaked with every step he took, and the headmaster, after a brief glance at them, silently nodded to the boy to take his seat. Elvira couldn't help but think how different it would have been had Miss Allison still been there. She would have been really happy for Clarry and would have told him how smart the boots looked. All that Mr Christmas could think about, however, was the fact that although the fête had been cancelled he must still give the school a holiday since so few of the pupils had brought dinners with them.

"What's come over old Flintstones, then?" Elvira grinned as she caught up with Clarry in the playground after school, "Melted her heart, have you?"

"Wasn't Flintstones bought my boots, Elvie," Clarry declared, his eyes popping. "You'll never believe it, either! It was that friend of yours. That Miss Kindness. She comes walking up the driveway this morning, large as life, along with the rector. Caught old Flintstones on the hop too. She was still in bed!"

"Miss Kindness brought you those boots!" Elvira repeated incredulously. "But how did she know where to find you? Or the size of your feet? How did she know you even wanted boots?"

"Well, now! I reckon maybe that was the old gentleman's doing," Clarry smiled. "Remember when we went up the attics? I took my boots off once to try on some old wooden clogs and I saw the old gentleman pick one of them up. Staring at it real hard, he was. I couldn't think why."

Elvira shook her head wonderingly. "She is a rum 'un that Miss Kindness!" she commented, sounding for a moment very much like Rhoda. "But with a heart of gold, that's for sure. And her dad, too. So! No more rainy-day holidays for Clarry Rae," she finished with a chuckle as they sloshed through the little rivulets running down Factory Hill.

"That's right," Clarry agreed with a heartfelt sigh of contentment. "Reckon I can even go out this afternoon no matter how hard it rains. What about going up to the house? We could get on with the inside cleaning," he suggested.

"Good idea," Elvira told him. "I couldn't bear to be shut in with Rhoda and Arthur all afternoon. Not with Rhoda acting all moody."

"Meet you down at the end of the track then. About two," Clarry called cheerfully as he strode off through the Old Rectory gates and along the gravel path, the triumphant crunching of his new boots sounding to Elvira like faint, short bursts of applause.

15

'There's someone in there!'

When Elvira announced she was going out that afternoon, Rhoda stared at her.

"Whatever can you find to do out of doors in this weather?" she asked. "It's toppling down!"

"Oh, this and that," Elvira answered, reddening. "I daresay I won't melt."

"I daresay you won't!" Rhoda retorted waspishly. "Only I hope you're not getting into any mischief. Seems like you can't stay at home nowadays. And Mrs Fisher says you don't play with the St Peter girls any more."

"Mrs Fisher should mind her own business." Elvira scowled, lifting her damp raincoat from the hook behind the scullery door.

76

"The woman was only concerned about your welfare!" Rhoda exclaimed. "Suppose you stumbled on one of these spies in your wanderings. What would happen to you, then? A slip of a girl! And all on your own!"

"Well, I'm not on my own! I'm with Clarry Rae, if you want to know," Elvira replied impatiently. "And we're not doing anything wrong. We're making something," she added with sudden inspiration.

"Artie want to make something, too!" her little brother shouted, scrambling to his feet from the muddle of toys that surrounded him on the rug.

For a moment Elvira stood with bated breath. What would she do if Rhoda insisted that Arthur go with her? She couldn't possibly take him up to the Sanctuary! She needn't have worried though. Rhoda was too concerned for her little boy's comfort to allow him out on such a wet afternoon.

"There now!" she petted him, taking him up on her knee. "You'll go with Elvie and Clarry another time, when it's not raining. He can, can't he, Elvie?"

"I suppose so," Elvira replied without much enthusiasm.

Outside it was as though the whole countryside had been relinquished to the rain, for the roads and the fields were equally deserted. Yet the air was full of sound as every hedge-row and tree poured forth the songs of countless, invisible birds.

"Pretty jewels! Pretty jewels!" the song thrush seemed to be carolling about the raindrops that hung like diamonds from every branch. "No more buckets! No more buckets!" Elvira's heart sang back joyfully as she skirted the muddiest parts of the St Peter road.

Elvira expected to find Clarry waiting for her when she arrived at the end of the goosegrass path but there was no sign of him. She was about to walk on towards the Old Rectory when she heard a single shrill whistle from the coppice and saw Clarry emerge about halfway up the track.

"Frightened of the rain?" Elvira teased, as she squeezed through the fence and ran up the slippery path to join the boy.

77

" 'Course not!" Clarry retorted. "I was hiding from that long-nosed Sophie Christmas. I bumped into her just as I was coming out of the Old Rectory gates. She's out looking for the spy, so she says! And she followed me all the way up the hill."

"How d'you get rid of her?" Elvira asked as Clarry began to lead the way up the slope.

"Chased her with a frog," he called back over his shoulder.

"Oh! Poor, little old thing! That was real cruel!" Elvira scolded as they arrived at the top of the field and turned left into the coppice.

"Thought you couldn't abide Sophie Christmas," Clarry said indignantly.

"I can't," Elvira exclaimed. "I feel sorry for the poor little frog! Enough to change it back into a tadpole seeing our Sophie at close quarters!"

Clarry's delighted guffaw rang out.

"Hooked me there, good and proper, didn't you . . ." he was saying, when his voice suddenly faded and he halted abruptly gripping Elvira's arm. They were about to emerge in the meadow that lay between the coppice and the Sanctuary, and at the very moment that Elvira turned enquiringly towards her companion, she heard what had perturbed him. For faintly but unmistakably the sound of music was floating over from the house!

"It's that piano again!" Clarry whispered, his eyes enormous in his thin face. "Like what I told you about. Remember, Elvie?"

Elvira nodded. She listened intently, then after a minute she said, "I don't think it's a piano, Clarry. Sounds more like bells to me. Pretty little bells."

"Doesn't matter what's making the music!" Clarry hissed. "Shows the place is haunted, just like I said! I don't like it, Elvie. It's giving me the creeps!"

But Elvira who had been staring hard at the Sanctuary now gave a little gasp. "There's someone in there, Clarry!" she exclaimed. "I saw them pass by the parlour window. Twice. I'll swear it!"

"A human being?" Clarry asked uncertainly.

"Looked very much like it!" Elvira replied quietly. Then after a moment she turned to look at her friend intently. "You sure you haven't told anyone about this place, Clarry?" she asked.

" 'Course I haven't!" Clarry shot back, his face flushing with indignation. "You didn't need to ask that, Elvie. You ought to know that."

"Sorry," Elvira apologized, looking back frowningly at the house. "It's just that I thought someone might be playing silly tricks." Clarry's eyes kindled. "Oh, yes!" he breathed. "I see what you mean, Elvie. Perhaps someone followed us up here without us knowing. Sidney Spurgeon and his gang, maybe!"

Elvira shrugged, her expression despairing. Whatever the answer, it was the end of the Sanctuary, that was for sure. With someone else in on their secret her dream of making the house into a hideout had been destroyed.

But Clarry was intent only on the present situation, his face hardening into a rock-like determination. "I'm going over there to flush them out! Whoever they are!" he suddenly announced. And, before Elvira could protest he was loping through the glistening grasses of the meadow towards the house.

"Wait!" Elvira called in alarm. For she knew that Clarry was hot-headed enough to run pell-mell into danger without taking the slightest precaution. Indeed he had bounded through the front door and was already in the lilac parlour before a breathless Elvira caught up with him. Apart from the two of them, however, the room was empty and silent.

"Nobody," Clarry shrugged, looking questioningly at Elvira. "But I did see someone," Elvira faltered.

"And we heard that music, didn't we?" Clarry added.

Each silently wondered whether they had been deluded by some trick of the imagination. As they stood there, in the throes of indecision, the house seemed to fall about their ears.

It started with an almighty crash. Then a tinkling of breaking glass from somewhere up above. Simultaneously the plaster began to fall like rain from the ceiling of the room on the other side of the hall. They clutched each other, their terror robbing them of the power to speak or even to think. Then slowly, very slowly, Elvira's numbed brain began to function.

"I know what that is!" she burst out all of a sudden. "It's that mirror, Clarry! That big mirror in the room upstairs. It's fallen over."

"Been knocked over more likely!" Clarry rasped back. With two bounds he was out of the room and hammering up the stairs.

"Oh Clarry! Do be careful! Those steps . . ." Elvira yelled in alarm.

But her warning came too late. Even as she ran out into the hall, Clarry's right foot, in its steel-tipped boot went clean through the rotten tread of the seventh step, the splintered wood tearing at his trousered leg so viciously that he let out an agonized howl.

"Clarry! Oh! Whatever have you done?" Elvira wailed, as she saw the blood soaking through the boy's grey sock.

But Clarry, now half sitting on the unbroken end of the step, made no reply. He was staring up towards the top of the stairs with an expression of horror on his white face. And Elvira, following his gaze, saw why. They were no longer alone. A figure was standing looking down on them. Nor was it Sidney Spurgeon or anyone else they knew. It was a man! A tall man with spiky, yellow hair, and he was wearing a grey uniform.

"A German!" Elvira whispered unbelievingly, and she went limp and cold with a chilling terror such as she had never experienced in her life before.

Her first instinct was to run — run for her life! But then she heard Clarry give a little, choking sob and she knew she couldn't leave him; not lying there with his injured leg at the mercy of a vicious Hun!

"Don't worry, Clarry," she said tremulously. "Whatever happens, we'll be together." Then she sank on to the bottom step, buried her face in her hands and waited for the worst.

80

16
Bill

"Don't be afraid," the prisoner said quietly in English. Then, after a moment, added, "I won't eat you, you know. Not today, anyway. I had my dinner not so long ago."

Elvira raised her head cautiously. The German had come down as far as the third step, and she could see that he had pinned a sack around his shoulders, as the farmworkers did, to keep off the rain.

"What you doing here?" Clarry suddenly asked in a jerky little voice that told Elvira how scared he was.

"Hiding," the man replied with a wry smile. "Or trying to before that mirror became troublesome." His smile faded though, as his eye fell on Clarry's bleeding leg. "Your wound should be cleaned," he went on. "If we went downstairs perhaps I could help."

"NO!" The horrified refusal came not from Clarry, but from Elvira. Only the previous week Mrs Honeyball had been telling her how a German, disguised as a doctor, had poisoned a whole ward of British Tommies in an army hospital.

The German sat down on the edge of his step with a sigh, and for the first time Elvira noticed that he was a young man — older than Thomas Crow perhaps, but much younger than her dad.

"I really can help your friend, you know," he said, looking earnestly at Elvira. "I am studying to be a doctor, you see. I can clean that nasty gash for him and bandage it up. Also I think he may have sprained his ankle a little."

"I have and all!" Clarry put in tautly, bending over to unlace a boot that was already tightening around his swelling foot.

"In that case," the German continued, "we should attend to that immediately. *May* I help?" he asked again almost pleadingly.

"Yes," Clarry replied without hesitation.

"But, Clarry!" Elvira began, standing up with a little wail.

" 'S all right, Elvie!" the boy assured her irritably. His face was yellowy-white now, and he was clenching his fists and scowling hard to keep back the tears. He looked down at his blood-soaked sock, then up at the German. "Can't think how you're going to clean it, though," he said chokily. "There's no water here. Nothing!"

"Ah! You wait and see!" The young man stood up and began cautiously descending the stairs, testing each tread before he put his weight on it. When he reached Clarry he stepped neatly over the boy then, to Elvira's horror, turned swiftly to scoop him up in his arms.

"Oh, don't hurt him!" she cried out involuntarily.

"Don't you worry, little Elvie! This friend of yours is a feather! I will not drop him," the German called cheerfully as he negotiated the remaining six steps.

Elvira, pressed against the front door, felt the hairs rise on the nape of her neck as the German said her name. What right had he to call her Elvie? A Hun! An enemy soldier! She glared at him resentfully, feeling as though he had taken some precious belonging of hers without her permission.

The German, however, appeared not to notice her animosity and smiled at her as he carried Clarry through to the lilac parlour. After a moment Elvira followed, standing uneasily to one side, as the man lowered Clarry to the floor so that his back was against the wall. He then carefully proceeded to remove the boy's boot and sock. She watched the German's fingers, long, sun-bronzed and rough from fieldwork, gently poke around Clarry's ankle and she shuddered. How could Clarry bear to have a Hun touch him like that! It was horrible! But Clarry, eyes screwed tight shut now in his thin, white face looked as though he didn't much care what was happening to him.

The German pulled a small stone water-bottle from his back trouser pocket and set it on the floor. Then he suddenly stood up and strode over to the hearth. Elvira, from her station beside the door, stared hard. For the man was inserting what looked like a piece of wire into the lock of the cupboard beside the gouged-out fireplace — the cupboard that neither Elvie nor Clarry had ever succeeded in opening. Now, as the door pulled open, Elvira gasped and the young man swung round.

"Yes! I'm having to give away all my secrets today," he smiled. "But since it is in such a good cause, I don't really mind."

When he came back to kneel by Clarry he was holding a yellow oilskin packet from which he pulled some squares of lint and rolls of bandages that looked as though they had been made out of old sheets.

"The ankle first, I think," the German muttered. Liberally sprinkling two pieces of lint with water from the bottle, he positioned them on either side of Clarry's swollen, red ankle and firmly and expertly began to bandage the boy's foot.

"Cor! That's better! Loads better!" Clarry exclaimed, as the young man tied the final knot and tucked in the ends of the bandage.

"Good!" The German looked up at Elvira then and nodded towards the open cupboard. "There is a large, thick book in there, Elvie," he said. "Will you bring it over and we can use it to prop up Clarry's foot? It is *The Collected Works of William Shakespeare*, and the good rector has loaned it to me. But I'm sure he won't mind if it supports Clarry's ankle."

"Reckon we ought to know your name," Clarry ventured, as the German began to wipe the dried blood from the long cut on his leg. Elvira, still maintaining a disapproving silence, knew that Clarry was deliberately avoiding her eye.

"You can call me Bill," the young man said to Clarry as he drew a flat tin of ointment from the oilskin package. "That is what my friends over here in England call me."

"Like Kaiser Bill?" Elvira put in acidly.

The German raised his head, and considered her for a moment with calm, blue eyes. "In a way," he said eventually. "My name is Wilhelm Ehrlich, you see. But from when I started studying medicine in London I have been 'Bill' to all my fellow-students."

"You lived in London!" Clarry exclaimed in amazement, as

Bill set about bandaging his ointment-smeared leg.

"For three years," the young man smiled.

"And now you want to kill us all, do you?" Elvira rasped out, dark eyes smouldering.

"No, young lady! I do not want to kill anyone!" The German sprang to his feet looking more annoyed than offended. "I do not want to kill," he repeated. "Not now! Not ever! My chosen profession is that of mending people. Not of breaking them into pieces!"

"Then why are you in the German army?" Elvira demanded.

"Because, Elvie, I had absolutely no choice," Bill replied quietly. "I was home in Germany on vacation when the War broke out. One minute I was picnicking in the forest with my little sister, Siggi. The next I was in an army barracks. It was like a nightmare."

"What battles were you in then?" Clarry asked eagerly, ignoring Elvira's poisonous look.

"Only one, thank heavens!" the young man answered. "It was near Mons, in Belgium. That was where I was captured. So you see I have spent all this stupid war in prison-camps. I am not a real soldier at all!"

"Elvie's dad's gone missing in France," Clarry blurted out, glancing uneasily up at his friend.

"Oh, no! I am so sorry," Bill declared, turning to Elvira with a face that looked genuinely grieved. "How many in your family?" he went on to ask. "Is there just you and your baby brother?"

"How do you know about Arthur?" Elvira demanded shakily, feeling an icy chill of apprehension begin to steal over her.

"Don't you remember?" the young man laughed. "I gave him a little car I had made. One day last winter. That was the first time I saw you, Elvie. The second," he added, "was up at the church. I was playing the organ while you sat outside with the rector. So I almost feel that I know you by now."

Elvira took a step back. "What I want to know," she said flatly, "is what you're doing up here in the Sanctuary. You're

84

supposed to be a prisoner!"

"And so I am a prisoner — most of the time," Bill said ruefully, walking over to gaze through the dusty window against which the rain was drumming. "But I found a way out of the grounds of our camp. Quite by chance. And also by chance I found out about this house. As soon as I saw it I knew what it was going to mean for me! An opportunity to have a little privacy again. To read. To smoke a cigarette. To think what I will do when the War is over . . ."

"But don't they miss you?" Clarry put in, puzzled.

Bill shook his head. "They are not too strict in this camp. In the evening we are free to wander about the building. If I am not in the dormitory they think I am in the common room or the laundry. As long as I am there before nine-thirty, which is bedtime, I think I will be safe."

"And this afternoon?" Elvira enquired.

Bill shrugged. "It is raining. No fieldwork. Everyone sleeps. The guards play cards. No one will miss Ehrlich for an hour or so." Then, suddenly wheeling round, he looked at Elvira curiously. "Why did you call this house the Sanctuary a moment ago?" he asked.

"Well, you see," Clarry broke in eagerly, "Elvie wanted to get away from Arthur and her stepmother. And I wanted to get away from old Flintstones that runs the home where I live. So when Elvie found this place . . ."

"She had the same idea as I had!" Bill finished for him with a smile. "She saw that this could be your sanctuary too! And this is why you have been so busy with your brooms and shovels! Now I understand. So! Perhaps we can share our sanctuary?" he suggested softly.

"Why not!" Clarry exclaimed. The colour had returned to his face and he was his normal, bright self again.

But Elvira was not to be so easily won over. "What about that music we heard this afternoon then?" She frowned. "What kind of trick was that?"

"Music? Oh, ho! Yes! I know what you mean." With a shout of laughter Bill had bounded over to his cupboard again to withdraw a small, polished wooden box. He held it up for them to see, then lifted the lid and a pretty bell-like tune came floating out.

"Of course! A musical box!" Clarry exclaimed in disgust. "Why didn't we think of that, Elvie?"

After a couple of minutes the young man gently closed the lid. "This is very precious to me," he said quietly. "I have managed to keep it with me for almost four years. You see, I bought it for Siggi's birthday. It is her favourite tune — *The Lorelei*, it is called. About a water-spirit that lures poor sailors to their doom. But they hauled me off to the army before I had a chance to give it to her."

"What age is your sister?" Elvira asked, dropping her guard for the first time.

"Siggi? She is almost fourteen now," Bill sighed, his blue eyes growing sad. "I have missed four years of her growing up. We have no parents, you see," he added. "And Siggi lives now with a dragon of an aunt. So it is very worrying for me."

Elvira nodded, visibly thawing. Here was a situation and an anxiety that she could understand and that made the German, for the moment, seem neither alien nor an enemy.

Bill looked at them both, smiled briefly, then picked up the oilskin package and carried it over to replace it in the cupboard. The water-bottle he shoved back in his pocket.

"I must go now," he announced. "It is not wise for me to stay away too long in the afternoon. Clarry, you must rest your foot a little longer, until the swelling has gone down. Then you should be able to walk. But don't disturb the bandage for four days at least. The dressing on your leg, though, you must change night and morning. Will you remember that?"

"Yes, Doctor Bill," Clarry grinned. "What about old Shakespeare?" he asked, pointing to his foot-prop.

"Just leave him on the floor," Bill told him. "I will find him next time I come up. Perhaps I will find you, too," he added, "since I no longer have to scuttle away into my little holes when you both march in! I have very much enjoyed talking to you," he finished, with a little bow. "Goodbye, little Elvie, goodbye, Clarry."

" 'Bye, Bill!" Clarry called warmly, as the German prisoner vanished.

But the murmur that came from Elvira could have meant anything.

17
Spying Glasses

"Go on then!" Clarry urged, as he limped stiffly behind Elvira through the coppice. "You've got to say! Do you like him or don't you?"

Elvira stopped, plunged her hands into the pockets of her waterproof and leaned back wearily against the slender trunk of a birch. Ever since the German prisoner had left them an hour ago Clarry had been going on at her. Nagging. Asking the same question. Until now she was on the verge of yelling at him.

"Look!" she said irately. "What does it matter what I feel about him? Fares you like him well enough for both of us."

"So I do like him then," Clarry admitted. "But we're mates, aren't we? So it's only fair you should tell me how you feel, Elvie. Else I won't know where I stand."

Elvira stared beyond Clarry into the green, dripping tranquillity of the trees. "He's a German," she brought out at last. "He's our enemy. It's wrong to like him."

"No, he's not!" Clarry shot back defiantly. "Look how he fixed my leg up. And he doesn't want to hurt English people. He said so. Didn't you believe him?"

Elvira, pinned down, wriggled, but was forced by Clarry's challenging stare to answer directly. "Yes," she confessed reluctantly. "I do believe that — that he doesn't want to fight."

"So he isn't our enemy!" Clarry proved triumphantly.

"But he is a German," Elvira persisted.

"And if you didn't know he was a German you'd like him better than . . . Mr Christmas. Wouldn't you now?" Clarry demanded, the glint of victory in his eye.

Elvira was forced to nod.

"Or Sophie Christmas? Or Mrs Fisher? Or Flintstones? Or even Dr Fletcher? Honestly now, Elvie?"

"Yes! All right," she conceded irritably.

"Well, then! We can't blame our Bill because of Kaiser Bill and his nasty gang, can we?" Clarry asked reasonably as Elvira turned away and started walking again.

"I wish you'd shut your mouth and let me think a bit!" she called back rudely.

The trouble was that Elvira was feeling horribly muddled. For it was true that she had liked the German prisoner. Right from the moment when he had started to talk about the musical box and his young sister. His face too, was the kind that Elvira always felt you could trust. Neither too smiling nor too stern and with clear, thoughtful-looking eyes. Altogether, in fact, the young man reminded her quite remarkably of her own father. But then in spite of all that, wasn't he still a German? And hadn't they all been taught for the past four years that no German was to be trusted?

Elvira walked out of the coppice and came to a halt at the top of the goosegrass path. The rain pattered on her hood, reverberating in her ears like tiny drums. Clarry, limping to her side, shook her arm and said loudly, "Bet your dad would like Bill. Bet he wouldn't care that he was a German."

Elvira whirled round, startled. "My dad!" she repeated.

Clarry nodded. He looked unusually solemn, and stubborn too. Elvira, staring at him, knew all at once that he was right. She had talked a lot about her dad to Clarry. About the way he fought for people's rights. And how he was always going on about all men being brothers. And about nationalities and class not being important. And now Clarry in an uncanny way, had come up with a truth that swept away all her doubts. For he was right! If Dad had met Bill he would have liked him. And it wouldn't have mattered a jot to him that Bill was a German.

"All right, Clarry," she sighed with a resigned smile, "I do like German Bill. And perhaps it doesn't matter that he is a

German. Still, he has rather put an end to us becoming 'The Children of the Coppice'," she couldn't help adding.

"I don't see why!" Clarry remonstrated, his face clouding. "Bill wouldn't bother us, Elvie. Only coming up for an hour or two like he does."

"But the Sanctuary was to be a secret hiding-place," Elvira protested. "That was the whole point of it."

"Well, it's Bill's secret hiding-place, too!" Clarry exclaimed. "And he won't give us away. Same as he knows we won't tell anyone about him."

Elvira pushed her hood back from her ears as though this might help her to think more clearly. Then she said, "All right. We'll go on as we planned then, Clarry. We'll keep working on the Sanctuary. Only no one down there," she pointed vaguely in the direction of the Frissingtons "had better discover we've even talked to a German or we'll be shot!"

"They'll never find out," Clarry told Elvira cheerfully, leaning on her shoulder for support as they started down the slippery path towards the road. "I can't come up tomorrow evening," he added. "I've to help old Flintstones clean out the kitchen. But I could come Friday. What about you?"

"Might as well," Elvira agreed. "I'll be stuck in evenings when Rhoda goes back to work. So I might as well make hay . . ."

". . . while the rain pours?" Clarry finished with a grin.

Elvira gave a derisive snort as she helped the boy through the wire fence and down on to the road. "Pity you weren't as sharp earlier on this afternoon, Clarry Rae," she commented. "Then you wouldn't have gone falling through those stairs and — making a fool of yourself."

And with a gurgle of triumph at having the last word, Elvira raised her hand in a farewell salute and went splashing uphill towards home.

It seemed now as though the rain would never cease. All through Wednesday night it hissed and rattled and drummed on roofs and windows. For a brief half-hour on Thursday morning a pale sun peeped wanly out then retired abruptly, like an invalid who has overtaxed his strength. By the time Elvira started on the road to school the rain had resumed with increased vigour. She could see the little Larters, swathed in sacks, hopping on ahead of her and the sacks reminded her of German Bill. What would he be doing at that moment, she wondered, as she passed the Old Factory. How did the prisoners spend their days when they were unable to work out of doors? She had never thought of this before.

The school attendance always suffered when it rained heavily for more than a day, since many Frissington families had problems drying clothes. Today, by the time Elvira arrived, only about half of Standard 6 had turned up and these were gathered in an excited bunch in front of the headmaster's desk. As Elvira hung her dripping coat on the hook at the back of the room, she could see that Mr Christmas hadn't yet arrived, but that Sophie was presiding in his stead. What was most surprising though, was that Sophie appeared to have her school-fellows' undivided attention.

Flora Crack wheeled to greet Elvira as she wandered up to the back of the group. "You'll never guess!" she whispered, her eyes shining with excitement. "That Sophie Christmas's gone and found the spy's field-glasses! That's them in the brown case, sitting on old Happy's desk. Constable Appleby's coming in to talk to us about them in a minute."

Clarry, scarcely limping at all now, had come in close on Elvira's heels. He pushed in between the two girls to ask, "How does old Sophie know they're the spy's glasses?"

" 'Cause they're German ones," Flora replied.

"Where did she find them?" Elvira was asking, when the sudden appearance of the headmaster and P.C. Appleby sent the pupils scattering to their seats. Only Sophie lingered, leaving the dais with obvious reluctance, but her grandfather was too preoccupied to notice her.

Constable Appleby removed his helmet and his dripping cape before stepping up on to the dais. He was a cheerful-looking man with a red face and old-fashioned side-whiskers, and he succeeded in remaining cheerful-looking while he told them the details of Sophie's dramatic find. Sophie Christmas, he explained, had used the previous afternoon's holiday to do a bit of detective work — to see if she could find any clues about the identity of the spy suspected of working in the neighbourhood. And just by chance, at the end of the afternoon, she had decided to take a peep into the old ruined barn in Rectory Close, up at the top of Factory Hill. There, just inside the doorway, had been the brown leather case containing the field-glasses! Very powerful and expensive field-glasses too!

"But please, sir! How do you know they belong to the spy?" George Pollitt shot his hand up to ask.

"Well now! You look at this, my lad!" The constable unbuckled the straps of the leather case and held it high so that they could all see the name printed inside it.

"L-E-I-T-Z," Constable Appleby spelled out carefully. "Now I don't know rightly how to pronounce that. But it's the name of the maker. And I expect you've guessed by now it's a German name. And if you look a bit further down inside here, you can see the name of the shop where the glasses were bought. And that's in a German city called Frankfurt. So I don't think there's much doubt as to who these glasses belong to."

"And I expect the children are wondering why the glasses should have been lying in the old barn, constable," Mr Christmas put in, pointedly consulting his pocket-watch.

"Ah, yes," P.C. Appleby continued in the same leisurely fashion. "Well, it would seem to me that whoever owns these glasses had to hide them in a hurry. Most likely because he'd been disturbed. So he had to stick them under the first bit of cover he could find. And what I'd like you all to do is to try to recall whether you've seen anyone recently acting suspicious-like up near Rectory Close. Think hard. And if you remember anything then let me know."

"Please, sir! Do you mean a stranger?" Sidney Spurgeon asked, darting a nervous glance at Mr Christmas as though afraid his question might be ridiculed.

But Constable Appleby didn't smile. "Not necessarily, lad," he replied quietly. "And whatever anyone reports to me will be treated as confidential. So don't be afraid to come forward."

Then, with a final beam of encouragement, the constable relinquished the dais to the headmaster and, having picked up his cape and helmet, took his leave of them, the field-glasses tucked beneath his arm.

"Well! What do you reckon to that then?" Flora Crack turned to enquire of Elvira. "It's made me feel all queer and trembly inside!"

Before Elvira could reply though, Mr Christmas raised his hand to silence the murmur that had arisen in the classroom.

"Yes, yes! I know how you must be feeling," he said solemnly. "It is not a pleasant thing to know for certain that we do have a spy in our community. There is one bright aspect of the affair, though. That is the fact that we have all been shown this morning how much even one young schoolgirl can contribute to the defeat of the enemy — if she is conscientious and alert, and willing to sacrifice even a holiday afternoon for the sake of her patriotic duty."

Sophie Christmas looked around self-importantly, with a smile like that of Alice's Cheshire cat almost splitting her thin, freckled face in two!

"Tell you what! I'm beginning to feel proper sick myself now," Elvira muttered to Flora.

18

Where's Clarry?

When Elvira arrived home on Thursday afternoon, she found Rhoda repacking her dad's parcel. Mrs Fisher, it appeared, had suddenly produced a writing pad which had been buried under some other pre-war stock in the back storeroom.

"Like gold, writing paper is out at the Front," Rhoda

observed to Elvira as she tied the string firmly around the parcel again. "Your dad will really appreciate this — whenever he gets it," she added, a trifle waveringly.

"Heard about the field-glasses then?" Elvira asked, hastily changing the subject, for Rhoda tended to become very prickly once she started worrying about her husband.

"Haven't we just!" Rhoda raised her eyes ceilingwards. "Mrs Fisher was full of it, of course. I'll swear Artie and I had to stand half an hour waiting to be served this morning! And then later on we had a proper commotion up here in Frissington Angel. P.C. Appleby arrived in a car with two army men. Turned out Mrs Diaper and Mrs Larter had both seen a strange man wandering around the Mitchells' windmill on Tuesday afternoon!"

"No! Truly?" Elvira gasped, a shiver chasing down her backbone at the idea of the sinister Frissington spy having been so close to them. For the Mitchells' old windmill stood in the sloping field behind the farmhouse and could be clearly seen from Frissington Angel green.

"Yes. Only it turned out he was a gentleman from Ipswich come to inspect the old mill for Mr Mitchell and tell him whether it was safe or not," Rhoda laughed. "So the spy-catchers were disappointed."

"Oh!" Elvira didn't know whether to feel relieved or deflated.

"Reckon everyone in the Frissingtons should put their heads together and see if they can't trap the varmint," Rhoda remarked as she opened the door by the fireplace to go upstairs with the parcel.

"Except that P.C. Appleby seems to think it might not be a stranger," Elvira said.

"Then he's dafter than he looks! Which one of us Frissington folks is likely to be in touch with Kaiser Bill, I ask you!" Rhoda sniffed scornfully as she disappeared.

"Bill, Bill, fell down the hill!" Arthur chanted happily as he emptied his barrow-load of soldiers out on to the rug.

Elvira listening to him bit her lip thoughtfully. For Arthur's little nonsense song had resurrected a worry that had been niggling at her for most of the day. Ever since P.C. Appleby had talked to them she had been thinking about German Bill and how he was able to slip out of the Camp undetected. And though he didn't seem as though he'd be connected with spies, Elvira couldn't help wondering whether she and Clarry ought to report what they knew of him to the constable. She made up her mind to talk to Clarry about it as soon as possible.

"Elvie play with Artie!" her little brother suddenly demanded with what he considered a most ferocious growl.

Elvira laughed and dropped to her knees on the rug, very soon forgetting her own worries in the imaginary battles and struggles of Arthur's tin soldier armies.

Friday morning dawned chilly as well as wet. Before Elvira left Rhoda had reluctantly lit a small fire with a shovelful of their precious store of coal as the wood which they used for their cooking-fires burned too fast to warm the room effectively. At school too the tortoise-stove was roused from its summer slumbers, but only to belch swirls of choking smoke into the classroom because the wind was in the east. Mr Christmas's good humour was extinguished along with the stove and Standard Six was sentenced to wrestle with decimals for most of the morning.

"Wish I hadn't come in!" Lizzie Pitt whispered to Elvira. "Mam wanted me to stay home and mind the baby. Wish I had!"

"Me, too!" murmured Elvira. Not that she meant it. She would have hated to have stayed at home all day with Rhoda and Arthur.

"Wonder where Clarry Rae is," Elvira mused a little later on. She had been intending to buttonhole him at break, but it was already ten-thirty and his place was still empty.

"P'raps that old Flintstones has run off to Bingham Market to pawn his new boots," Lizzie suggested, her normally solemn face alight with inspiration.

"Yes, maybe," Elvira agreed without conviction.

Clarry didn't appear that afternoon either and on her way home Elvira discovered from the Coopers that none of the home boys had been at school that day. Flintstones has probably taken one of her funny turns, she decided. She's probably kept them in all day as a punishment . . . or maybe even as a treat! She would find out from Clarry that evening if he came up to the Sanctuary.

For a precarious half-hour after tea though Elvira almost gave up hope of escaping to the Sanctuary herself. Rhoda was in a black mood and had started complaining as soon as Elvira had arrived home from school. There was a pile of wood to be chopped and a whole heap of mending to be done, Rhoda declared. And Elvira was no help at all. If she didn't have her nose stuck in some silly book she was out running wild with that daft Clarry Rae!

"There's nothing wrong with Clarry!" Elvira said fiercely. "He's my friend. And I'm meeting him again tonight. So there!"

"Oh, no you're not, miss!" Rhoda had rasped out, drawing herself up to her full height and staring down at Elvira with hard, black eyes.

By seven-thirty, though, Rhoda had finally been worn down by Elvira's sulky silence and had told her abruptly that she could go out if she wanted to. "Only don't blame me if you catch your death! It's bitter tonight!"

Elvira, far from feeling cold, was in a welter of perspiration by the time she arrived at the Sanctuary as she had run most of the way. She barged in through the front door in a shower of raindrops calling Clarry's name as she did so.

"Hello!" a cheerful voice called back from the room on the right. But it wasn't Clarry's voice. It was the German prisoner who appeared in the hallway holding a sweeping-brush and a shovel. "Clarry is not here," he informed Elvira. "Only me. I have been helping with the housework, sweeping up some of the plaster that fell from the roof the other day."

"Whatever can have happened to Clarry?" Elvira burst out,

more taken aback by her friend's absence than by the fact that the German was there.

"You had an arrangement to meet him?" Bill asked, catching the anxiety in Elvira's tone.

Elvira nodded, flushing guiltily as she remembered the reason for her eagerness to talk with Clarry. To hide her confusion she said quickly, "He wasn't at school today, either."

"Perhaps he is sick," Bill suggested. Then added anxiously, "I hope his leg has not been troubling him."

Elvira shook her head. "No, it's not that," she said. "None of the boys from the home were at school today."

"Poor Clarry!" Bill remarked unexpectedly and turned to walk back through into the living-room.

Elvira followed him. "Why do you say that?" she asked, looking up into the young man's solemn face.

Bill considered for a moment. "This home where Clarry lives is not a good place, Elvie," he replied at last. "The boy is suffering from what is called 'malnutrition'. That means . . ."

"I know what that means," Elvira cut in. "It's not having enough proper food to eat so that you get ill. My dad told me that. Will Clarry get ill then?" she finished anxiously.

"He might," Bill replied with a sigh. "It is sad. He is a charming lad. His smile is like sunshine."

Elvira looked around the empty room and her eyes began to glow. She was envisaging it furnished with an old chair or two. Perhaps some coloured cushions and rugs picked up at a jumble-sale, and with a log-fire crackling in the hearth.

"I'll see he eats properly when we move in here," she burst out. "We'll have our own vegetables and hens. Maybe even a pig."

Bill's eyebrows shot up. "So? You intend to live here!" he exclaimed. "I thought your plan was just to escape here like I do. A few hours at a time. But actually live here! Well! That is an adventure."

"Just until the War is over," Elvira explained. "Until my dad comes home." Her voice trailed off uncertainly as it tended to do nowadays whenever she mentioned her dad.

"Tell you what!" the young man suggested suddenly. "Why don't I help you with the house-cleaning this evening for a bit? I could reach to the high places — the ceilings, the tops of the walls. Would that be useful?"

"Yes. That would," Elvira agreed readily. She felt a surge of friendliness towards the young man and with this feeling of warmth came the conviction that whoever the Frissington spy might be, Bill could have no connection with him. She had no need now to discuss the matter with Clarry. "Tell you what," she said, "if you like to scrape some of that mildew from the walls, then I can start on the hearth. I should think we'll need shovels and scrubbing-brushes."

To begin with they worked in a companionable silence. Then as Bill laid down his brush for a moment to wipe the perspiration from his brow he said, "My goodness! These walls are really thick with dirt. I wonder how many years it is since the manager and his family left here."

Elvira, on her knees before the hearth swung round. "The manager?" she repeated, puzzled.

"Yes. The manager of the silk factory whose home this was," Bill replied.

"How ever did you find that out?" Elvira was astonished and Bill could not restrain a smile.

"Not by black magic, I assure you," he replied. "It just happened that I found a large plan of the old silk factory rolled up in a cupboard in the medical room one day when I was cleaning it. This house was marked clearly as belonging to the manager. There was a long driveway which led through those trees out there and down to the roadway."

Elvira nodded slowly. "Yes. That makes sense," she said. "Clarry and I couldn't figure out why this house was built up here all on its own. Or why it had been abandoned either. Clarry thought there might have been a murder or something."

"Clarry sounds very like my Siggi," Bill remarked with a chuckle. "She also has a vivid and bloodthirsty imagination."

Elvira was studying Bill curiously. "Is that how you found a

97

way out of the Camp then?" she asked suddenly. "From the old plan?"

But Bill shook his head. "Oh, no," he explained. "That was quite another accident. I had been watching the guards play football one day round at the back of the building. The ball kept hitting against the wall . . . you know, that high ivy-covered wall that runs right around the grounds?" Elvira nodded.

"Well, I began to notice that when the ball hit one certain part of the wall it made a different sound. Deeper. More hollow. So when the game was over I went to investigate. And there, beneath the thick curtain of the ivy I made my discovery . . . a wooden door!"

"Open?" Elvira gasped.

"Oh no," Bill laughed. "Very closed! With a lock that was all rusted up too. But I worked on that whenever I could with grease and oil and finally I managed to open it with a piece of wire. I am very good at opening locks with pieces of wire," he finished, eyes twinkling. "It was a skill I learned when I was a small boy. I never knew how useful it would be to me one day."

Bill worked for half an hour longer and then said he must go. "I have enjoyed myself very much," he told Elvira, pausing for a moment in the doorway before he left. "It reminds me of the old days when I would help Siggi make her dreams come true." His voice faded just as Elvira's had done when she had talked of her dad.

"I expect we'll be here again on Sunday afternoon," she said eagerly. "Will you be here too?"

"If it rains," Bill smiled. "Otherwise we have to work on the land. But I will say in German, '*Auf wiedersehen*', Elvie. That means, 'I hope to see you again'."

"Owf veeder-sing," Elvira echoed and was rewarded by a delighted shout of laughter from the departing Bill.

Later on the way home, she repeated the odd-sounding phrase over and over. Skipping to it down the goosegrass path, jumping to its rhythm over the puddles on the road. When she arrived home Rhoda came bursting into the scullery to meet her. "Well, you haven't been out tonight with Clarry Rae. That's for certain!" she greeted Elvira.

"No. He didn't turn up . . ." Elvira faltered, her cheeks starting to burn. For a moment she had an insane urge to turn and run back out into the rain. She knew that if her stepmother were bent on an inquisition she hadn't a hope of evading her questions. But it transpired that Rhoda was eager not to elicit information but to hand it out.

"You'll never guess, Elvie!" she went on excitedly. "Ivy Honeyball's just called in. And you know that Miss Flint at the home?" Elvira nodded.

"Well! They came and took her away this morning!"

"Who took her away?" Elvira asked.

"The police!" Rhoda exclaimed. "They've taken all the boys back to London and they've shut up the Old Rectory."

"But why? Why've they done it?" Elvira gasped.

"Can't you guess?" Rhoda asked. And as Elvira shook her head she went on, "Because she's the spy, of course! That Miss Flint is the Frissington spy!"

19

A Fading Rainbow

Inevitably Elvira was shocked by the news of Clarry's abrupt departure. But in common with everyone else in the Frissingtons, she felt a profound relief that the spy had been removed from their midst.

It was to be a short-lived relief, however. For at eight o'clock on Saturday evening Elvira, running out of Mrs Fisher's shop with their week's ration of bacon, almost collided with the Reverend Robson-Turner. The rector, who was carrying a small overnight bag, looked tired and bedraggled, his boots and trouser-legs spattered with mud.

"Hello, Elvira," he smiled wearily. "Your expression tells

me that I look a fright. I've just walked from Bingham Market railway-station and been splashed by every vehicle that passed me. Has it been raining here all day?"

Elvira nodded and then asked, "Having a bit of a break, were you, Rector?"

"Oh, no," the rector replied hastily. "I was accompanying the home boys back to London, Elvira. You heard about them moving, of course?"

"Yes," Elvira replied, her face clouding at the thought of her friend being so far away. "Still," she added with a sigh, "I suppose we ought to be grateful that the spy's been found at last."

The Reverend Robson–Turner pushed his cap back from his brow, and a raindrop trickled down his long, thin nose. "Spy, my dear?" he repeated, looking mystified. "What spy is this?"

"Well, Miss Flint, of course," Elvira replied. "That is why they took her away, isn't it?" she added, suddenly uncertain.

"Miss Flint! Oh no! No, my dear!" the rector exclaimed. "The home was temporarily closed on the recommendation of an officer of the Society for Prevention of Cruelty to Children — an officer brought here by the efforts of your friend, Miss Kindness, as a matter of fact. I had been trying for a long time to have the Flint woman removed, but the home authorities just wouldn't listen."

"So she wasn't the spy after all?" Elvira gasped.

"I'm afraid not, Elvira," the rector replied as he moved off. "It's a perpetual puzzle to me how these absurd rumours ever start!"

"Well, it wasn't Mrs Fisher to blame this time." Rhoda assured Elvira when the latter had told her stepmother of her conversation with the rector. "Funnily enough she was the only one who wouldn't believe the Flint woman was the spy. Said she was much too lazy and stupid. Seems she was right, too! But imagine that Miss Kindness getting the home closed and all!" Rhoda added admiringly.

"Yes. I expect she noticed Clarry was suffering from malnutrition," Elvira remarked without thinking.

"Was he?" Rhoda asked, looking shocked. "Who said so, Elvie? The rector?"

"No . . . yes . . . I can't really remember," Elvira stumbled, her face reddening as she saw Rhoda's eyes grow curious. "Anything I can do this evening?" she asked hurriedly. And her ploy worked.

For Rhoda quickly reached beneath the sofa to pull out her pillowcase full of mending and decided which articles she could delegate to Elvira and which she would have to attend to herself.

The rain continued on Sunday in a series of heavy showers alternating with feeble bursts of sunshine. Rhoda, who had been struggling with a headache all morning, lay down on the sofa after dinner and was soon fast asleep. Little Arthur was intent on some imaginary game with his old pink rabbit so Elvira, thinking the moment favourable for her escape, tiptoed into the scullery where she grabbed her coat from its peg and fled. As she hurried along the deserted, muddy road her thoughts reverted sadly to Clarry. Where was he at this precise moment, she wondered? And what would he be doing? Would he be missing the Frissingtons? He would be missing his friends, at any rate. It seemed odd to be going to the Sanctuary knowing that Clarry might never appear there again. Elvira was bursting to tell Bill the news of the home's closure. It was the way she felt when she had something important and exciting to tell her father. Something that she knew would matter to him as much as it did to her. For in a strange way she knew that the German would really care about Clarry's welfare and his future.

"EL-VIE! . . . EL-VIE!"

Elvira was halfway up the goosegrass path when a high, wailing cry from behind made her spin. To begin with she could see no one, Then, down on the road at the foot of the track a small, white-pinafored figure suddenly rose upright.

"Oh, no! Artie!" Elvira gasped in dismay as she started a

mad, slithering race downhill. Arthur, who must have followed her from the cottage, had been prevented from crossing from the road into the field by the half-filled ditch.

"Oh, Artie! You naughty boy! You're wet through!" Elvira scolded as she hoisted the bedraggled toddler into her arms and set off towards home.

"Artie want to play wif Elvie!" he sobbed on her shoulder, overcome as much by his failure to achieve his goal as by the cold discomfort of his clinging, wet clothes.

Once home, Elvira wakened Rhoda, gave her a brief explanation of Arthur's escapade and then slipped away again as her perturbed stepmother rushed her son upstairs to change his clothes. By the time she finally arrived at the Sanctuary it was four o'clock.

"Come in here, Elvie! I'm finding wallpapers now," a happy voice hailed her from the living-room. Elvira hurried in to find Bill pointing to the faint outlines of sunflowers that were beginning to appear beneath his energetically-wielded scraper. "No Clarry again," he informed her with a frown. "You have news of him?"

Elvira, removing her wet coat and sitting down cross-legged on the hearthstone, launched into a breathless recital of Miss Flint's dismissal and the removal of the boys. Bill listened intently, nodding his approval.

"But that is wonderful!" he exclaimed at last. "Not that you have been separated from your friend, Clarry, of course. But that the children have been rescued in time, Elvie. Children without parents are at the mercy of so many harsh forces in this world."

The thought that she herself might by now be an orphan popped for a dreadful moment into Elvira's head. But she chased it away resolutely. "When did you lose your parents, Bill?" she asked quietly.

The young man sat down too with his back against the wall, facing Elvira. She noticed for the first time how extremely shabby and frayed his grey uniform was. "It was ten years ago," he told her. "I was fourteen. And Siggi was just four.

102

Our parents were musicians. My mother was a violinist and my father a pianist. They travelled all the time to give concerts while we stayed at home with our grandfather. There was a terrible railway accident just before Christmas and they were both killed. Our grandfather died three years later, and then we went to Aunt Berthe who was my father's sister-in-law. She is a real dragon!"

"What does Germany look like? Is it like Suffolk?" Elvira asked.

"Germany? Ah . . . well, it is a very big country," Bill explained with a smile, "and it contains many different kinds of scenery. But where we have always lived is a very beautiful part. It is in the Taunus Mountains quite near Frankfurt."

"I've heard of Frankfurt," Elvira put in, frowning as she tried vainly to remember where she had encountered the name before.

"Aunt Berthe's home is in a village called Schöndorf," Bill went on. "It has steep, winding streets and tall houses with red roofs that glow in the sunlight. There are hundreds of cherry trees. And in many of the gardens there are tables with umbrellas where the summer visitors can eat when they come on trips from Frankfurt. High up the mountain-sides there are forests of fir and larch-trees, and down in the valley there are orchards and strawberry-beds, and peaches growing against the sunny walls of the houses."

"Oh! It sounds beautiful!" Elvira breathed. "I would love to see it."

"Perhaps you will," Bill said gently. "One day when this wicked war is over, Elvie, you will maybe come to spend a holiday with us. I have a feeling that you and Siggi would become good friends."

"Tell me about Siggi," Elvira urged.

"Siggi . . ." he began thoughtfully. "Well . . . she is quite tall. Up to my shoulder the last time I saw her. She has hair coloured like mine, only it is very curly. Like little corkscrews all over her head. Aunt Berthe is forever trying to flatten it down! She has blue eyes, and a small, turned-up nose. And a smile that really shines out at you."

"And what sort of things does she like doing?" Elvira asked eagerly.

"Let me see," Bill murmured. "Ah, yes! She adores to run barefoot through the forests. She likes climbing trees, and caring for orphaned creatures — animals, birds, even snakes — which sends dear Aunt Berthe into hysterics. She reads books. Swims. Listens to music."

"And what doesn't she like?"

"Being shut indoors on a sunny day. Being bossed around. Having Aunt Berthe stand over her while she practises her piano music." Bill smiled.

Elvira nodded. She was satisfied. Now Siggi was more than just a name. "I don't know much about music. But I like hearing you play the organ in the church," she said after a moment. "I was imagining it was Frissington's golden angel singing."

"Golden angel?" The young man looked puzzled so Elvira quickly related the angel legend as Miss Kindness had told it to her.

"But that is a wonderful story!" Bill exclaimed when she had finished. "I shall tell it to Siggi in my next letter. She will love it. She will sit and dream of where the angel might have been hidden. But now! Back to work!" he added decisively, springing to his feet so suddenly that he knocked over the long-handled broom, which he had propped against the wall. The resultant bang sparked off a flurry of activity in the wall behind Elvira, and Bill looked down at her.

"That sounds like rats." He frowned. "Have you made plans to deal with them before you move in, Elvie?"

"I wanted to leave them in peace," Elvira replied a little doubtfully.

"A kind thought," Bill remarked, "but not very practical, I'm afraid. Rats and mice carry disease, Elvie. Perhaps we should start thinking about how to evict them."

An anaemic sun was blinking through the window an hour later as Elvira rose to look critically down at the square of floor

104

she had been scrubbing. "It's such slow work," she sighed.

"But rewarding," Bill said encouragingly. He was standing by the door, about to leave. Elvira looked across at him, another thought occurring to her. "Would you mind having a look at the well before you go?" she asked. "Clarry and I couldn't think what to do with it. But perhaps you will."

Bill's efforts to move the massive plug of concrete that blocked the well-mouth were, however, just as ineffectual as Clarry's had been. "Oh, dear! No!" he gasped eventually, staggering back to lean against the old apple-tree. "It will need superhuman strength to move that, Elvie."

As Elvira, downcast, turned away, Bill let out an exclamation. She turned back to find him pointing delightedly at a great double rainbow that was spanning the sky.

"Look, Elvie! How beautiful!" he breathed. They stood perfectly still for a minute, united in a reverent, admiring silence. Then slowly and inevitably the rainbow began to fade.

"So!" sighed Bill, when the sky was once more as grey as his own drab uniform. "*Auf wiedersehen*, little Elvie. I will see you next week perhaps."

Elvira nodded. She raised her hand in a little gesture of farewell as Bill went off, but she didn't move. She was staring at the grey sky, her heart suddenly heavy with doubts and misgivings. So many problems seemed to have cropped up. Clarry's disappearance from the scene. The question of the rats and mice. The impossibility of unblocking the well. For the first time since the idea of the Sanctuary had occurred to her, she saw how ambitious it had been. And not only ambitious – unrealistic, too. Like a child's dream. Or a rainbow, Elvira reflected, as she started slowly towards the coppice. A beautiful, insubstantial rainbow that eventually fades to leave the world just as grey as it had been before.

20
Rhoda Makes Enquiries

As Elvira returned home from school the following afternoon old Mrs Boniface suddenly came hurrying down her path brandishing a black umbrella with Arthur trotting at her heels.

"Strike's over!" she called to Elvira breathlessly. "They came for Rhoda at ten o'clock this morning, dearie. She said to tell you to boil the rabbit bits and the roly-poly pudding."

"Yes, Mrs Boniface. Thank you," Elvira said politely, waiting until Arthur came scampering over to grab her hand.

"Looks like that's never going to leave off raining now," the old lady grumbled as she turned away. "And that's turned bitter cold now an' all. More like winter than summer!"

Rhoda said much the same that evening as she made another tick on the calendar that hung to the right of the fireplace. It was the twenty-first tick she had made since they had first received news that Elvira's father had gone missing.

"The twenty-fourth of June!" she sighed. "And who would believe it! Look out there, Elvie. It's only nine o'clock and it's real dark and gloomy. We'll have to light the lamp, even if it does mean using up some of our paraffin. There's still a heap of mending to be done." Just as they had settled down at the table with the mending spread out between them there was a loud tap at the back door and P.C. Appleby poked his head into the scullery.

"Sorry to disturb you, Mrs Preston," he called pleasantly. "But I'm afraid that lamp's shining out a bit bright through your curtains. And you know what the regulations are!"

"Oh, Lord!" Rhoda exclaimed, jumping to her feet. "I clean forgot! I've put up my summer curtains. And they're thinner than the winter ones. Shall I put the lamp out?"

"Oh, no! No call for that," the constable chuckled. "If you just dim it down a little and move it up this end of the table, that should be quite satisfactory." Rhoda hastily did as P.C. Appleby suggested then, still a trifle flustered, asked him whether he would care for a cup of tea.

"That I would, Mrs Preston!" the policeman said, stepping forward with alacrity into the living-room. "I feel proper chilled this evening."

Elvira, by no means reluctant to leave her mending, set about making the tea, while Rhoda continued to sew and chat to their visitor.

"No more traces of our spy then?" she enquired.

"Well . . . Mr Mitchell thinks he might have seen someone signalling from the church tower last night," P.C. Appleby told her. "But there was a bit of lightning flickering about the sky at the time. So he's not certain sure."

"Nasty business it is," Rhoda sighed. "I felt proper relieved when they said it was that Miss Flint. Pity it hadn't been!"

The constable nodded, smiling his thanks to Elvira as she handed him a weak, but steaming, cup of tea. "Just been up to the Old Rectory now, as a matter of fact," he confided. "That's not going to be empty much longer," he added meaningly before taking a sip of his tea.

"You mean the boys are coming back?" Elvira asked, her face lighting up.

But the policeman shook his head. "No, my dear. Not your young friends. Other 'boys'. The boys that have been fighting for us out at the Front. Wounded lads from local regiments. They're coming to the Old Rectory to convalesce."

"From local regiments?" Rhoda's head shot up, her needle falling disregarded on the table. "When are they expected?" she asked.

"Tomorrow teatime, I believe," the constable replied. Rhoda nodded and sat lost in thought for a while before she picked up her needle and resumed her work. As soon as P.C. Appleby had gone she turned to Elvira. "I'm going down there, Elvie," she informed her stepdaughter tautly. "I'm going to go and ask if I can speak to every soldier there! See if any of them have heard any more about your dad. Don't you think that's a good idea?"

Elvira, startled by the urgency in Rhoda's tone, looked up

and saw the ray of hope in her glowing, dark eyes. "Yes," she said quietly after a moment. "I think it is a good idea, Rhoda. It can't do any harm at any rate."

Rhoda returned from her visit to the Old Rectory at nine o'clock on Wednesday evening during a violent thunderstorm. Elvira, who had been lost in the tribulations of Rosalie, the twelve-year-old heroine of *A Peep Behind the Scenes*, bumped back to reality to find her ashen-faced stepmother standing beside her.

"What is it, Rhoda? Not bad news about dad?" she whispered, frightened by the other's expression.

Rhoda shook her head and sat down slowly in the fireside chair. "No news at all about your dad," she said dully. "There was no one there that knew him."

"Then what is it? What's wrong?" Elvira demanded.

Rhoda looked up at her and swallowed hard before speaking. "Oh, Elvie! They're such poor souls!" she burst out tremulously. "When you see them like that. All together. Just boys most of them. Some without legs. Others without arms. And then the blind ones! Oh, it's horrible! Horrible, Elvie! If I thought that would ever happen to Artie . . ." All at once she dropped her face in her hands and began to weep.

Elvira went over to put a hand awkwardly on Rhoda's shoulder. "There now!" she said after a moment. "Don't upset yourself, Rhoda. I'll make you a cup of tea and you'll feel better presently."

But Rhoda remained in low spirits for the next two days. Indeed so quiet and dull was she that Elvira found herself wishing that she would flare up occasionally in her normal quick-tempered fashion. Even little Arthur looked at his mother strangely from time to time as though trying to puzzle out what was wrong with her. Then on Saturday morning Rhoda complained of feeling unwell. Too unwell to go to work. "My head's aching something fierce!" she groaned, standing before the range with her fingers pressed against her temples. "And horrid, icy shivers keep running up and down my back. My throat's sore too."

"Best go back to bed, then. I'll fetch the water and start the washing," Elvira said, casting an anxious glance at her step-mother's flushed face. Apart from having an occasional head-ache, Rhoda was never ill.

By that Saturday lunchtime, however, it was obvious that Rhoda was, for once, really ill. She wanted nothing to eat or drink, and she was drenched in perspiration and complaining of bad pains in her back and legs. "Don't let Artie in here, Elvie," she whispered hoarsely. "It might be catching. And he's too little to throw things off like us."

Elvira nodded. "He can play out of doors, anyway," she said cheerfully. "It's turned ever so warm and sunny again. A wonderful drying day."

In actual fact Elvira was already quite enjoying her tempor-ary role as mistress of the house. She liked deciding when the meals were to be dished up, and mothering Arthur, and telling him stories while she ironed the clean, crisp laundry. She didn't even regret missing her Saturday excursion to the Sanctuary.

" 'Spect your mam will be better by tomorrow," she told her little brother, as she tucked him into his cot that evening. "Then you'll be able to go in and see her. She's too tired tonight."

By Sunday morning Rhoda was considerably worse and Elvira rushed, panic stricken, across the green to the Diapers. "Oh please! Could you go in your trap and fetch Dr Fletcher for me?" she gasped, as the startled-looking blacksmith opened the door to her frantic knocking. "Rhoda's so queer! She's breathing ever so quick. And she doesn't seem to know who I am!" Half an hour later Dr Fletcher came downstairs from Rhoda's room to where Elvira was waiting anxiously with Arthur on her lap.

"Tell me, my dear," he began, frowningly, "has Mrs Preston had any occasion to be up at the Old Rectory recently? Any errand, or . . ."

"Yes," Elvira broke in. "She went up there Wednesday night, Doctor, to see if she could get any news of my dad."

Dr Fletcher closed his eyes, gave a deep sigh, then nodded slowly several times. "That's it then. Just as I feared," Elvira heard him murmur.

"What is it?" she demanded. "What's wrong with Rhoda, Doctor? Is it bad?"

"Yes, my child. I'm afraid it is rather bad," Dr Fletcher said, his face softening as he looked down at Elvira and Arthur. "Mrs Preston has caught an illness that the soldiers have brought home with them from France. It is a nasty, new disease. They're calling it 'the Spanish Influenza'. She's very ill. I can't pretend otherwise. And she will probably remain so for some time. I'll be back presently with some medicines. And I'll see if I can find some help for you," he finished more cheerfully.

After the doctor had gone Elvira settled Arthur on the sunny, back doorstep with his bowl of bread and milk. Then she hurried upstairs to bathe Rhoda's forehead with tepid water. Watching her, Elvira felt herself being sucked into a black morass of panic. She had never felt so terrified, alone, and helpless in her life.

Not long after Dr Fletcher's return with Rhoda's medicines, however, a familiar-looking motorcar drew up outside the Prestons' gate and Miss Kindness came hurrying down the path with a small suitcase in her hand! Dr Fletcher had apparently called on the rector to see if he knew anyone who might come to Elvira's aid.

"The Reverend Robson-Turner telephoned me, and here I am!" Miss Kindness beamed at an incredulous Elvira. "I'll have to go to work every day, of course. But I can share chores and the night-nursing with you, my dear."

Elvira stood quite still, biting her lip, before she managed to mumble, "Oh, I am so glad you've come, Miss Kindness! I just didn't know what I was going to do! It's ever so good of you!"

"Nonsense! What are friends for if they can't lend a hand in a crisis?" Miss Kindness retorted briskly, as she laid her hat on the table before following Elvira upstairs to the patient's room.

Just before noon as Elvira was laying the table for lunch, she heard a delighted whoop from Arthur out in the front garden. She crossed curiously over to the window, and her eyes shot wide open!

"Mr Robertson from the bookshop! And Mrs Robertson, too!" she exclaimed, watching the elderly couple clamber down from their pony trap. "Whatever can they want?" She soon found out.

"We drove over to Frissington St Peter chapel this morning," Mr Robertson informed Elvira, "and as soon as we learned about your predicament we decided to come up right away and take little Artie back home with us. If he'll come, that is . . ."

Arthur had always been fond of Mrs Robertson and he was already snuggled up on her lap in the fireside chair.

" 'Course he'll come!" Mrs Robertson cooed. "Won't you, Artie? Come for a little holiday to Auntie Robbie's? And play with the new puppy? And Fluffy the cat? And ride on the pony?"

"Mam and Elvie come, too?" Arthur enquired doubtfully.

"Not for the moment, my lamb," Mr Robertson said gently. "Just Artie. Do you know there's a swing in our garden? And a little stream where you can sail paper boats? Would you like to do that?"

There was no need for any further persuasion. Arthur was already scrambling to the floor, eager to leave. Elvira rushed upstairs and hurriedly gathered together the little boy's clean clothes. She tiptoed into Rhoda's room to tell Miss Kindness what was happening. "Do you think I should waken Rhoda to let her say good-bye?" she whispered.

"No, dear. She wouldn't understand, anyway. Her fever's too high at the moment," Miss Kindness said softly.

So Elvira stood by herself in the sunny road waving hard after the little pony trap as it vanished down the Frissington St Peter track. As she turned to go back into the cottage, Mrs

111

Honeyball called her to ask how Rhoda was.

"She's caught the Spanish Influenza," Elvira informed her. "Dr Fletcher says the soldiers have brought it back from France."

Mrs Honeyball retreated a few paces, an expression of alarm on her round face. "The Spanish Influenza!" she repeated. "Well! That's a new one to me!" And she hurried indoors to tell Mr Honeyball the name of the new disease that was soon to have the Frissingtons in its deadly grip and would eventually affect two hundred million people all over the world.

21

Influenza

Rhoda remained seriously ill and delirious for nearly two weeks. During the day Elvira had to sit by her side almost constantly, pulling her upright when she was overcome by a spasm of coughing, changing her poultices, persuading her to take her medicine, and occasionally a tiny sip of brandy as Dr Fletcher had directed. Rhoda had brief periods of lucidity, when she would ask about Arthur or whether any news had come from Elvira's father. But mostly she looked at Elvira with strange, blank eyes, then turned her head away to ramble incoherently.

More than a dozen people in the Frissingtons had gone down with the influenza and many mothers were keeping their children indoors to prevent them catching it. On balmy July evenings when Frissington Angel would normally have resounded with the calls of playing children, the green was deserted and there was an unnatural silence.

"It doesn't seem right, somehow," remarked Elvira one evening, "that the weather should be all bright and summery when Rhoda and all these other folks are so poorly."

"No," Miss Kindness agreed with a sigh. "It's altogether too much. As though this never-ending war weren't enough to contend with . . . And the food shortages and strikes all over the country. We could have done without this pestilence — indeed we could!"

"Rhoda's not going to die, is she?" Elvira asked suddenly.

"No. She is not," Miss Kindness said firmly. "I should think she'll be very poorly either tomorrow night, or on Saturday. Then her temperature should fall and she'll begin to pick up."

And so it turned out. On Saturday afternoon Rhoda's fever suddenly heightened, so Miss Kindness took a nap on the couch downstairs in preparation for an all-night vigil at the patient's bedside. When Elvira tiptoed into Rhoda's room on Sunday morning she found her stepmother sound asleep and breathing normally for the first time in a week. "She's over it," whispered a tired Miss Kindness. "She's as cool as a cucumber now."

"That woman is well named," Rhoda remarked in a weak, little voice to Elvira on Monday morning as they listened to Miss Kindness's car stutter away from the gate. "What would we have done without her, Elvie? She really is an angel."

"Yes, she is," Elvira agreed. "And she's determined to stop with us for one more week, Rhoda, so don't you be getting up out of your bed or trying anything foolish. You've been ever so ill, you know!"

"Don't worry, Elvie," Rhoda smiled wanly. "I haven't the strength of a mouse at the moment and that's a fact. Still," she added with a sigh, "I shan't half be glad to have Artie back — even though he has settled so well with the Robertsons."

"Well, he'll be coming back next Saturday," Elvira told her, "so don't you fret about him. You must have a proper rest for a bit."

In the event though, it wasn't possible to bring Arthur home the following Saturday, for on Friday evening Elvira developed a sore throat and a pounding headache.

"You don't think Elvie's caught it now, do you?" Rhoda enquired of Miss Kindness in some dismay.

"It wouldn't surprise me," Miss Kindness sighed with a hand on Elvira's hot forehead. "It seems every house in the

113

Frissingtons has got a victim at the moment. The accursed thing's spreading like wildfire. They're having to shut down the factory from this evening because of it."

"But however will we manage? And what about Artie?" Rhoda wailed with panic showing on her white, drawn face.

"Leave little Arthur where he is, Mrs Preston," Miss Kindness said gently. "He's perfectly happy and so are the Robertsons. As for you . . . Well, I have a suggestion."

"Yes?" Rhoda said, looking a trifle suspicious.

"It's just that you're not fully recovered yet," Miss Kindness continued. "You need a spell of convalescence, and you're best out of the way while Elvira has this wretched illness. I want you to stay at my home, Mrs Preston. You'll have peace and quiet there and Molly and my father will be only too happy to have you."

"Oh, no! I couldn't," Rhoda exclaimed, looking shocked by the very idea. But Miss Kindness was firm and after a moment Rhoda quietly agreed. "Yes. All right then. Thanks very much. I will go — if it means I'll be back on my feet that bit sooner to look after Artie and Elvie."

"Good-oh," Miss Kindness exclaimed, and dashed off to make the necessary arrangements.

For Elvira the following week was a jumble of aches and pains and feverish nightmares. But with the devoted nursing of Miss Kindness she was soon on the mend and eagerly listening to snippets of local news that Miss Kindness brought back from Mrs Fisher's shop. The Spanish Influenza had apparently raged through the Frissingtons and not a household had escaped it. The German prisoners too had succumbed in a body. Down in Frissington St Peter several old people and three small babies had died, but as yet there had been no deaths in Frissington Angel.

"So perhaps that golden cherub is still in the neighbourhood watching over you all," Miss Kindness said to Elvira.

"I wonder if the spy's caught influenza," Elvira mumbled drowsily.

"Well, according to P.C. Appleby no one's seen or heard

114

anything for a week or two now," Miss Kindness replied. "On the other hand, I don't expect people have had time to watch for spies with all this dreadful illness about."

Elvira, raising herself a little on her pillows, opened her heavy lids to ask, "Are things any better at the Front, Miss Kindness? Have we won any battles?"

Miss Kindness shook her head despondently. "No, my dear," she sighed. "Things don't seem much better. They say the Germans have crossed the Marne now and are attacking Paris. Our only ray of hope is that the Germans are in a much worse plight than we are where food's concerned. They say they're on the verge of starvation and suffering terrible hardships."

"Oh, dear," Elvira whispered, her lids closing again as she drifted off into a doze. "I do wish something would happen to cheer us up."

And that wish, as Miss Kindness pointed out later, was granted very promptly. For the next morning a short letter arrived from Clarry Rae. Headed, 7 Meadow Park, Colegate, Surrey, it expressed the hope that Elvira was well and informed her that Clarry was now living with a Mrs Platt who was 'all right'. That the Platts' house was 'all right', and Mrs Platt's cooking was 'all right', but that Clarry didn't much like the local school or the local company. 'Tell Bill and Miss K. and her dad I was asking after them,' the letter finished. 'I miss you all. A lot!!!!! Yours truly, Clarry Rae.'

"And I miss him too, the great donkey!" Elvira sighed. Nevertheless, the letter brightened her up. She immediately asked Miss Kindness whether she could find her any paper and then sat up in bed for an hour writing an enormous letter to Clarry on the backs of old grocery bills. Coming to the end of her letter she wrote firmly, 'Miss K. says I can get up for a little tomorrow. So I will soon be out and about, Clarry. And as soon as I am, I will go up to you-know-where and hope to see Bill. Then I can find out how he has been and give him your message. Till then . . . all the best from your Friend and Partner, Elvie Preston.'

22

Back to Normal

Elvira did get up the following day, but only for a brief half-hour, morning and afternoon. The factory reopened that Tuesday morning and before going off to work Miss Kindness made Elvira promise that she wouldn't exceed her two half-hours. "Not that the weather's likely to tempt you out of doors," she remarked with a grimace, looking out of Elvira's window at the steadily-falling rain. "We shall all be growing webbed feet if there's much more of this."

It continued wet for the rest of the week, while Elvira's cotton-wool legs strengthened and her heart gradually ceased to bang in her ears whenever she climbed the stairs or made her bed. Elvira didn't mind being confined indoors, for now that she was feeling better she was able to enjoy reading without Rhoda nagging her to attend to some chore or Arthur demanding to be played with. The Kindnesses' family doctor had been worried that Rhoda might overtire herself if she returned home too soon and had advised her to stay on in Ipswich for a second week.

"Father could see she was worrying about little Arthur," Miss Kindness told Elvira on Thursday evening, "so he contacted Mr Robertson and had him bring the little lad over. I gather they're all having a whale of a time now, especially Molly, who hasn't had a toddler to fuss over for years!"

Elvira, her brow wrinkling, made some hasty calculations on her fingers. "A month!" she exclaimed eventually. "It's almost a month since I last saw Artie, Miss Kindness! It doesn't seem possible!"

"Yes," Miss Kindness sighed, glancing over at the calendar beside the fireplace. "It's the twenty-fifth today. We shall soon be into August and this rain's going to make the harvest very late."

But Elvira was staring at the calendar and at the twenty-five days of July which Rhoda hadn't been able to tick off. She stood up now, pulled open the table drawer to fish out a pencil and hurried over to rectify the omission. "Not that I'd forgotten about Dad. I think about him every single day!" she turned to explain defensively to Miss Kindness.

"Just as I'm sure he thinks about you too, my dear," Miss Kindness replied quietly.

Elvira crossed to the window to gaze out at the falling rain. "What's the latest war news, Miss Kindness?" she asked eventually.

"It seems the situation's much the same in France," Miss Kindness replied. "At home . . . well, a lot of idiotic people are starting up a grand witch-hunt of enemy aliens again. Wanting to shut people up in prison if their great-great-grandmothers came from Germany. That sort of thing. I can't think why. It's senseless, and very cruel."

"That's what Mr Robertson says," Elvira remarked, remembering the smashed window of Mr Price's shop in Bingham Market. "I expect it's people like Mrs Fisher that are doing it," she added. "I think she hates Germans more than anyone I've ever met!"

"I find that woman most unpleasant," said Miss Kindness. "She's definitely the person I'll miss least when I go home on Sunday, Elvira."

"Have you enjoyed being in Frissington Angel?" she asked.

"Indeed I have!" Miss Kindness told her earnestly. "My nanny was right. There's something special about 'angels', you know. They're a wonderful bunch of folks. A bit rough on the surface, some of them, but pure gold underneath . . . just like that lost, golden angel. You should be proud of belonging here, Elvira."

"Yet some people call Frissington Angel a rural slum," Elvira remarked, flushing as she recalled Sophie Christmas's comment.

117

"Then some people must have blocks of wood between their shoulders," Miss Kindness declared in scorn as she rose to put the kettle on for supper.

Rhoda too seemed to be looking at Frissington Angel in a new and favourable light when she arrived home with Arthur on Sunday afternoon.

"Oh, I *am* glad to be home, Elvie!" she exclaimed. "Not that dear old Mr Kindness and his housekeeper weren't wonderful to me. . . . But, well . . . home is home, after all. And there's nowhere else quite like it."

Little Arthur's joy at being home again took a more boisterous form as he hurled himself repeatedly at Elvira, then pulled out his toy box from beneath the sofa and greeted his favourite playthings with shrieks of delight.

"He'll soon settle down," Rhoda said, smiling as she and Elvira began to lay the table for Sunday tea. "By tomorrow morning it'll seem as though we've never been away."

This wasn't quite true though, for the experiences of the past month had made noticeable changes in both Arthur and Rhoda. Elvira found the new, gentler, quietly-spoken Rhoda a trifle disconcerting at first. And the change in little Arthur was equally startling. Living with the Robertsons for three weeks had 'brought Artie on no end' as Rhoda admiringly put it. He now insisted on feeding and trying to dress himself, and he had adopted many of the Robertsons' mannerisms and tricks of speech. 'Do you tell me that, now!' he would say in a tone of amazement when Elvira or Rhoda had made some quite ordinary remark. And when their laughter rang out, he would place his chubby hands on his hips and shake his head despairingly.

After two weeks' constant rain Monday dawned bright and sunny, and although the school had now reopened, Rhoda thought Elvira ought to have one last day's holiday and spend as much of it as possible out of doors. A month's absence from school had left Elvira with little inclination to return to the boring routine of the classroom and to Mr Christmas's hectoring. And without Clarry there to share her dinner-bag and discuss plans for the Sanctuary she was more than willing to remain at home for one more day and look after Arthur while Rhoda returned to work.

"Back to the old routine, then," Rhoda smiled at Elvira across the table, as they breakfasted together at seven o'clock. "I must say I feel quite glad about it, Elvie. I don't think I was meant to be a lady."

Elvira found herself sharing Rhoda's sentiments as she resumed all the old familiar chores. It was over a fortnight since she had last been out of doors and now, even crossing over to the farm for milk, or fetching water from the well gave her a little thrill of pleasure. Later on in the morning when she walked with Arthur down to Mrs Fisher's, she couldn't help stopping every few steps to listen to the birdsong or to gaze at the blue and yellow clumps of scabious and St John's wort now bordering the cornfields. When they reached the foot of the goosegrass path, she halted automatically and gazed up towards the Sanctuary, recalling with a pang how her dream of making the place into her own private refuge had disappeared. Still, she must go up there again as soon as possible to find out how Bill was and to give him Clarry's message.

"Artie want to go and play in the trees!" Arthur yanked suddenly on Elvira's arm, pulling her determinedly towards the brimming ditch which, once before, had barred him from the goosegrass path.

"Oh, no, he doesn't!" Elvira retorted. "He wants to fly down the hill like an aeroplane!" And she hoisted the little boy up in the air, swinging him downhill by leaps and bounds until he shrieked delightedly and forgot the forbidden delights of the coppice and the goosegrass path.

There were three customers standing in Mrs Fisher's shop when they finally arrived. Elvira's heart sank as she pushed the door open and heard the shopkeeper's penetrating tones. For Mrs Fisher was obviously delivering one of her tirades about the German prisoners and there was no knowing how long she might go on. "Twenty more of them arriving tomorrow!" she was declaiming. "And another twenty to come next week.

And do you know how much they're to be paid for helping with the harvest? Can you guess?" The three women shook their heads, but their faces were already darkening in anticipation.

"Six shillings and sixpence a day!" the fat shopkeeper spat out. "A sight more than our poor boys are getting in Germany, I'll be bound!"

"It's not right!" ferret-faced Mrs Groom put in.

"And on top of everything else there's the danger to us all!" Mrs Fisher continued breathlessly. "All these Huns in a small place like the Frissingtons. And the spy never caught yet, neither! We could all be exterminated in no time at all!"

The shopkeeper was wound up and would doubtless have continued had not Arthur ruined the dramatic effect of her monologue by suddenly piping up with an incredulous, "Do you tell me that, now!" This set the women shrieking with laughter and reminded a chagrined Mrs Fisher that she had a business to run. "Still home from school, I see!" she snidely remarked, as she took Elvira's ration-book from her. "Little Sophie Christmas still looks proper poorly, but she's gone back today."

"I can just imagine it!" Elvira remarked bitterly to Rhoda as she ironed her white school pinafore that evening. "Mr Christmas will be giving his dear little Sophie a medal for bravery and telling us all how wonderful she is. I wish I didn't have to go back tomorrow!"

Rhoda, who was jiggling Arthur on her knee, said, "We'd have the attendance officer on the doorstep if you didn't, Elvie. Anyway, I don't expect it'll be as bad as you think."

It was every bit as bad, Elvira thought morosely the following afternoon as she sat sleepily struggling with a sum about a woman buying yards of woollen cloth and silk. Judging from the muffled sighs and groans around her and the number of faces turned yearningly towards the classroom windows, Elvira could tell that most of her classmates were in the same plight as herself. Only Sophie Christmas was scribbling away industriously.

120

As Elvira's eyes wandered around the classroom she found herself unconsciously staring at Mr Christmas and saw to her horror that he was starting towards her to see what progress she had made. She was already tensing herself for the inevitable explosion when there was a tap on the classroom door, and the Reverend Robson-Turner came slowly in. The sound that swept through the room was like a soft gust of wind, composed partly of sighs of relief, partly of little shocked gasps. For the rector, who had almost died of the Spanish Influenza, was white-faced and stooped and walked with the aid of a stick. But as soon as he smiled at the children they felt reassured. He had come to ask them to save fruit-stones and nutshells which would be made into charcoal and used in the respirators that soldiers wore in gas attacks. Elvira caught up with him half an hour later on her way home from school as he was making his slow way up Factory Hill. He smiled at her, resting one hand on her shoulder and waving towards the valley with his stick.

"I've just been learning a lesson from those fields, Elvira," he told her. "Two days ago the oats and the barley down there were beaten flat by the rain. And look at them now! Erect and dancing in the sunshine! That's how it's going to be for us, too. I'm sure of it."

"Have you heard from Miss Allison lately, sir?" Elvira asked shyly as they started to walk on.

The Reverend Robson-Turner said that he had and that the headmistress couldn't wait to get back to her school. "She always asks after you especially, Elvira," he added kindly.

When they reached the gate of the Old Rectory where the rector was going to visit the wounded soldiers, Elvira remembered Clarry's letter and told the Reverend Robson-Turner what he had said in it.

"He's a good lad," the rector observed gently. "I hope he settles down in his new home. He deserves to be happy."

Then Elvira took a deep breath and asked the question that had been hovering on her lips ever since she had started talking with the rector. "The German prisoners, sir . . . I heard they'd

121

all gone down with the influenza, too. Are they all right, now? All of them?"

The Reverend Robson–Turner looked startled for a moment, then his face softened. "How kind of you to ask, Elvira," he said quietly. "No one else in the Frissingtons would dream of it . . . Yes, my dear," he went on, "they're all recovered now, though some of the poor lads had a very bad time of it."

Elvira beamed her relief as she waved good–bye to the rector and continued on her way. She wouldn't have dared to ask anyone else about the Germans. She couldn't imagine what would happen if anyone found out she was friendly with one of them! Bill was her friend. She was sure of that now. And she knew somehow that he would have been worrying about her during these past weeks, just as she had been wondering and worrying about him. As she hurried on uphill and past the Old Factory she resolved to slip up to the Sanctuary at the first opportunity.

23

A Helping Hand

It was Friday before Rhoda could be persuaded to allow Elvira out in the evening air. "And don't you be overtiring yourself or getting caught in a shower," she admonished her. "I'll need all the help I can get this weekend. Miss Penrose in the post office says the Robertsons have gone down with the influenza now. So I mean to go over to Bingham Market tomorrow afternoon and leave Artie with you."

"I'll take care, Rhoda! I promise!" Elvira called, grabbing her raincoat from its hook and skipping out of the back door before Rhoda changed her mind. As Elvira walked along she realized the wheat field would soon be ready for cutting. Then after the wheat would come the barley harvest, which Dad always hated so much because of the sharp little awns that stuck into one's skin. Experienced harvest workers always wore shirts with high collars when they were working with barley, Dad said. Any fool who worked bareback ended the day looking and feeling like a pincushion.

All at once a violent longing to see her dad again shot through Elvira like a stabbing pain. She sat down on her coat at the side of the path, swallowing repeatedly and pushing her fists hard against her eyes to prevent the tears from falling. If she could just picture Dad somewhere, it would help. In the trench with his mates. Or back at the camp playing football. Or marching along some muddy French road. It was the fact that he had just disappeared into nothingness that was so horrible. Even Rhoda had stopped looking for a letter from him now, though she insisted she hadn't given up hope of his still being alive.

"No news is good news, as far as I'm concerned!" she would say firmly to Elvira from time to time. Suddenly Elvira reached over and snatched a handful of ears of wheat, crushing them viciously between her fingers until the milky kernels fell on to the path, where she ground them with the hard, little heel of her boot. Feeling better, she rose and continued on her way.

The meadow around the Sanctuary was now gaudy with high-summer flowers, but the lilac and rhododendrons in the garden had withered to a dead brown. Elvira picked her way through the showers of tansy-gold and the blue pools of scabious. It's all changed, she thought sadly, looking around her and realizing that now she had no stake in this place, even in her dreams. Bill was in the lilac parlour sitting on the floor beside the fireplace with his back to the wall, smoking a cigarette. He hadn't heard Elvira come through the front door so was startled when she suddenly appeared before him. When he stood up, Elvira felt almost as shocked as she had been when the rector had walked into the classroom on Tuesday. For Bill was round-shouldered and gaunt-looking too, his shabby, grey uniform hanging loosely on him as though it were a size too large.

"Elvira!" he exclaimed, stamping out his cigarette and striding forward to grasp both her hands warmly. "I *am* glad you are all right! I have been so tempted to ask the rector about you! But I thought it best not to . . . for your sake."

"I'm glad you're all right too, Bill," Elvira replied shyly, walking over to perch gingerly on the ledge beneath the broken window. "You *are* all right, aren't you?" she added doubtfully, for once his welcoming smile had faded, Bill's face had become unusually sombre and there were deep worry-lines between his brows.

He looked at her for a moment, as though pondering how to begin, and then suddenly said, "Ach, I am so worried, Elvie! I cannot tell you how much! About Siggi and my aunt." He stuck his hands in his pockets and started to pace distractedly around the room as he explained. Amongst the batch of new prisoners who had arrived on Tuesday there had been a man whose home was near Frankfurt and who had received a letter from there just before he was captured. "He says things are so dreadful in our district, Elvie," Bill continued. "There is hardly any food now. And the Spanish Influenza is spreading through the villages. And there are no doctors left to care for the sick . . . I have had no word from home for two months now!"

Suddenly he punched the wall beside the window so hard that Elvira saw him wince with pain. She knew how he felt. It was exactly how she had been feeling a few minutes ago about her dad. Sad. And sore. But most of all, furious. Furious because there was nothing to be done but tear the heads off the wheat stalks, or bruise your hand against a wall. "I am sorry, Bill," she said earnestly. "I wish I could help."

Again he looked at her consideringly before he spoke. "Perhaps you can, Elvie." He turned away and started to pace round the room again. "Elvie," he said, slowly and clearly, "I am going to try to escape. I must get home to Germany. Will you help me? Please?"

"Escape?" Elvira felt the gooseflesh rise on her arms at the very sound of the word which conjured up darkness and danger.

124

"Oh, no! Please don't, Bill!" she said tremulously. "The War can't last much longer. Everyone says so."

"I can't wait, Elvie," Bill said, walking slowly towards her. "I must try to get to Siggi. You understand that, don't you?" She nodded reluctantly. "I have thought it all out very carefully," he went on reassuringly. "I won't take any stupid risks. I must get to a place on the coast called Walton-on-the-Naze. Do you know it?" Elvira shook her head.

"It's in Essex," Bill told her. "Not too far from here. And it's the best point from which to cross to Holland. I will have to try to find a boat there. It has been done before."

"But how will you get to this Walton place?" Elvira asked. "You're bound to be spotted. You're bound to meet people sooner or later."

"Yes. And that is where I need your help, Elvie," Bill replied, taking a deep breath and looking down unhappily at the toes of his worn boots.

"How? . . . How can I help you?" Elvira turned away and nervously started to trace patterns with her finger on the grime of the windowpane.

"There are things I need," Bill said. "A suit of working clothes, Elvie, like English countrymen wear. A little English money if possible. But most of all I need a reliable electric torch."

"Why? Because you'd be travelling at night?" Elvira queried.

"Yes. But also because there are things in the Camp that would be useful to me. For instance there is a cyclists' map of East Anglia in a cupboard in the medical room. But my only chance to get that will be in the early hours of the morning when I know the guard in the corridor has a little nap."

"When are you planning to go?" she asked.

"Just as soon as I can. As soon as I have the basic necessities," he told her. They stared at each other in silence.

Finally Bill said, "I know this is a very hard thing I'm asking of you, Elvie — to help an enemy of your country. For that is how everyone in the Frissingtons thinks of me."

"You're not my enemy," Elvira shot back, suddenly finding

her tongue. "Clarry and I settled that long ago. I've had a letter from him, by the way," she rattled on. "He's settled in a new place, but doesn't seem to think much of it. He was asking after you. Said to tell you."

Bill nodded, smiling gently. Elvira was sure he knew she was trying to avoid giving him a direct answer to his plea. He waited patiently until she had finished talking before he said, "So? Can you help me, Elvie? Is there any chance you can find a torch for me? Or any of the other things? The torch first, though. I really need that badly. This weekend, if possible."

Elvira listened for a moment to the evening serenade of a blackbird in the old apple tree beside the well. Then she said, "I can't decide right away, Bill. Not just this moment. I might be able to get the torch. And Dad's around your size. So his clothes would fit. But I'll have to think about it. Can you wait until Sunday afternoon?"

"You will bring me your answer then?" he asked her.

"I promise!" Elvira told him.

"Then I can wait," he said. "And thank you, Elvie for even considering my request!"

" 'S all right," she murmured, feeling embarrassed as she slipped off the window-ledge and made for the door. With Bill so polite and grateful she felt mean about not making her decision right there and then. "And thank you for trusting me," she added as she turned to give the German a friendly wave of farewell.

The parcel was on top of the wardrobe in Rhoda's room where it had lain for the past two months. It had been opened and repacked so often that Elvira knew its contents off by heart: a slab of chocolate, a tin of tobacco, cigarette-papers, a packet of raisins, a tin of antiseptic foot-powder, a tin of vaseline, and carbolic soap, the book from Mr Robertson's, writing paper, four pairs of socks . . . and an electric torch. A man at the factory had been selling the torches and Rhoda had been unable to resist buying one, even though she had wondered whether Dad would be allowed to use it. The torch had cost a pound and the three batteries one shilling and sixpence each.

Until well after midnight Elvira lay awake listening to Arthur's gentle breathing and turning Bill's request over and over in her mind. If only Clarry were here, she thought fretfully! It was so difficult to make a decision without talking the problem over with someone. Part of her wanted so badly to help Bill get back to Germany and to his sister. But another part kept recoiling at the thought that she might be acting as a traitor to her king and country. 'Aiding and abetting the enemy' – that's how helping a prisoner to escape was described. And that's what she would be doing if she took the torch intended for her dad and handed it over to Bill. Still undecided, but exhausted from wrestling with the problem, she finally fell into a troubled sleep.

It was a chance remark of Mrs Honeyball's that made up Elvira's mind for her the following morning. She was carrying the last of the water for the washing-copper across the green from the well when the woman waylaid her.

"Did you hear about Monday's fête being cancelled, Elvie?" she asked. "It's because of the influenza in Bingham Market. Seems they're afraid of it breaking out here again."

Elvira hadn't heard and she couldn't hide her disappointment. The Frissingtons' bank holiday fête was one of the highlights of the summer and so far it had managed to survive the War.

"Never mind, love!" Ivy Honeyball consoled her. "Just think how much worse off you'd be if you was a German. Says in the papers they're all going mad with hunger now. Eating grass and boiled shoes and all sorts," she finished as she turned away. "Serves them right, too! Wicked lot!"

As Elvira stood motionless, staring after Mrs Honeyball, she had a sudden vision of Siggi, curly-haired and blue-eyed, running barefoot through the trees. Siggi, whom she felt she knew, smiling at her, wanting to be her friend. Would Bill's young sister really be eating grass? Starving? Before she had reached the outhouse with the water, Elvira knew what she must do.

With Rhoda off to Bingham Market for the afternoon and Arthur playing out in the garden, Elvira was able to open her father's parcel at her leisure. To begin with she had only intended to take the torch and the batteries. Then thinking of the arduous journey Bill might have to face, she took out the chocolate, vaseline, and foot-powder as well. Darting through to her own room, she found a broken kaleidoscope and two large pebbles in the old toy box beneath her bed and she used these to fill out the hollows in the depleted parcel. No doubt Rhoda would discover one day that the items were missing. But by that time, with luck, Bill would be safely back in Germany. As for the terrible chastisement, that would fall on her own head . . . "Don't cross your bridges!" she whispered to herself sternly, standing on a chair to replace the parcel on top of the wardrobe.

"How can I ever thank you, Elvie?" Bill asked hoarsely, his eyes suspiciously bright as she handed him her booty the following afternoon.

"That's all right," she said, shrugging off his gratitude, but feeling pleased. "I couldn't bring the clothes today because Rhoda would have seen. What should I do about them?"

They were standing in the centre of the lilac-parlour in a golden pool of sunlight. "Do you think you could possibly come up here late next Thursday night?" he asked her slowly. "That is when I plan to leave, you see."

"How late?" she wanted to know.

"Midnight."

A little thrill of excitement and apprehension shuddered through Elvira at the prospect of the rendezvous. "Yes . . . all right," she agreed faintly.

"Bring the clothes with you then," Bill went on quietly, "and I can change here before I start out." He strode over to the locked cupboard beside the fireplace and opened it, laying the chocolate, vaseline and foot-powder on top of the oilskin package of ointment and bandages which he had once used to dress Clarry's leg. "I have always kept this stuff here just in case such an emergency ever arose and I had to leave," he explained. Then he locked the cupboard and walked slowly back to Elvira.

"Elvie," he said solemnly, "whatever happens to either of us . . . whatever is the outcome of this hateful war . . . I want you to know that I will always think of you as a very dear friend – both to me and to Siggi. I would like you to have this from us both."

He reached out and thrust into Elvira's hand the little musical box which she and Clarry had once listened to in terror from beneath the trees in the coppice.

"But I can't take this!" Elvira protested, looking down open-mouthed at the beautifully polished box. "You bought it for Siggi! And you've kept it for her all this while!"

"Please!" Bill said gently. "It is a gift of friendship. Siggi would want you to have it, too."

"Well . . . thank you, then! Thank you ever so!" Elvira said, her face radiant as she looked up at Bill. "It's very pretty. And I've never had a musical box before. I'll keep it safe and treasure it. Always!"

Later, as Elvira was making her way homewards through the coppice, she stopped to take the box from her skirt pocket and listen to its pretty bell-like tune. "I shan't be able to listen to it when there's anyone else about," she told herself. "I'll have to hide it, too. At the bottom of my old toy box where Rhoda's not likely to look." As she finally shut the lid down she turned the box over and saw the maker's name written in gold letters on the bottom. H. GUTMANN. FRANKFURT. Frankfurt? It was only then that Elvira remembered where she had seen and heard the name of the German town before. Of course! That was where the spy's field-glasses had been bought! The ones that Sophie Christmas had found in the barn in Rectory Close. P.C. Appleby had read the name out to them, then held the glasses up so that they could all see it. Funny that the glasses and the musical box should come from the same German town, Elvira mused as she sauntered on her way again. But then she didn't really know much about Germany. And come to think of it, she'd only ever heard of one other German city which was Berlin. Perhaps the Germans didn't have many towns, and lots of people travelled to this Frankfurt place to do their shopping. She would ask Bill, she decided, next time she saw him. At this thought a new and depressing realization suddenly dawned on her. The next time she saw Bill would be the last time! She was on the point of losing yet another friend. With a deep sigh she started to run, slithering and scraping down the flint-strewn surface of the goosegrass path, her hand clasped protectively around the smooth, little box in her pocket.

24

The Night of the Zeppelin

When Frissington Angel wiped the sleep from its eyes and squinted up at the sun on Monday the fifth of August, there was no indication that the day might turn out to be extraordinary. As it was a bank holiday most people had risen late and were moving about their chores in a desultory fashion. The cancellation of the fête seemed to have depressed the whole community, even old Grandpa Larter who came shuffling up to the farm dairy with his milk-can just as Elvira left.

"Don't know what you're looking so happy about," he grunted sourly.

"It's because I'm going to Ipswich today," she felt obliged to explain. "Miss Kindness is coming in her car to collect Rhoda and Arthur and me."

"Good luck to you then!" the old gentleman snorted as Elvira ran off. "Nasty, smelly old place Ipswich is! Wouldn't want to go there myself."

"Folks are just getting to the end of their tether, the old 'uns, too," Rhoda remarked forbearingly when Elvira told her what Grandpa Larter had said. "It makes them cross and spiteful.

Lucky we have a good friend like Miss Kindness to brighten us up a bit, Elvie."

Elvira nodded in wholehearted agreement. Rhoda had been about to put Arthur to bed the previous evening when the rector had suddenly appeared at the door, his face wreathed in smiles. It appeared that Miss Kindness had just telephoned him with a message for the Prestons.

"She heard about the fête being cancelled," the Reverend Robson-Turner explained, "and wondered whether you would like to spend the day with them. If you're agreeable she'll collect you at ten. But if that's not suitable I've to telephone back to let her know." Rhoda had thanked the rector profusely, overjoyed at the prospect of a day out and of taking Arthur to see old Mr Kindness and Molly again. Elvira's spirits soared too as she romped about the room with the exuberant Arthur. As soon as the rector had left, she and Rhoda had set about ironing clothes, polishing boots and laying out gloves, hats and handkerchiefs so that everything would be in readiness the following morning for their excursion. "I don't want any harassment at the last minute," Rhoda told Elvira firmly. "It's going to be a perfect day."

And that was how it turned out despite a change in the weather which brought an afternoon of showers and grey skies. Nothing could have damped the spirits of the Prestons, however. There was the treat of the car ride to Ipswich with Rhoda talking non-stop to Miss Kindness. Then at the Kindnesses' home lemonade and iced buns awaited Elvira and Arthur, with tea and scones for the adults. Later Arthur was introduced to the great red and black rocking-horse that had been brought down from the attic for him, while Elvira was turned loose in the library and exhorted to borrow whatever books she fancied. Lunch was a delicious combination of sausage-pie with onions and creamed potatoes followed by Molly's special chocolate blancmange. After lunch Miss Kindness whisked them all off to the village of Elmstow where she had heard there was to be a particularly good fête. They spent a delightful two hours watching the dancing displays, races and

Boys Scouts doing gymnastics. Best of all though, in Elvira's opinion, were the sideshows. Old Mr Kindness was particularly taken by the notion of kicking a football at a life-size effigy of Kaiser Bill, and he scored three hits in succession which earned him a jar of strawberry jam and the applause of the spectators.

By the time they arrived back at the Kindnesses' for tea, Arthur was looking sleepy, and on the drive home to Frissington Angel he fell fast asleep on Elvira's lap. Elvira herself was distinctly heavy-eyed as she shyly kissed Miss Kindness and thanked her for the marvellous day. By the time Rhoda had said her farewells she too was yawning widely.

"Artie in bed?" she whispered anxiously, as she came hurrying in through the scullery.

"He didn't even wake when I was changing him into his nightgown," Elvira informed her.

"It's all the excitement," Rhoda remarked, stifling another yawn. "A lovely day, though! Wasn't it, Elvie?"

"Lovely," Elvira agreed dreamily.

"And we're not going to need rocking to sleep, either!" Rhoda chuckled as she followed Elvira up the little winding stair to bed.

To begin with Elvira thought it was a bee caught in the lace of the curtain. Then as the droning became more insistent and heavier, her sleep-fogged mind began to clear a little. She didn't know what time it was, but she felt that she hadn't been asleep for long. Anyway, it was certainly very dark and bees didn't normally work a night-shift! She sat up and listened. The noise went on and on. It was rather like the engine of Miss Kindness's car when she left it running, or 'idling', as she called it. But who would have come up to Frissington Angel in a car at this hour? Her curiosity thoroughly roused now, she got up and tiptoed over to the window. There was nothing to be seen outside. It was slightly misty, but by peering hard she could see that the road outside the cottage was quite empty. The noise, however, went on, becoming louder with every minute.

With a quick glance at the peacefully-sleeping Arthur, Elvira headed for the bedroom door, determined to solve the mystery. Her bare feet pattered softly down the wooden stairs, and the door into the living-room squeaked irritably as she pushed it open. Although it was dark she made her way unerringly across the familiar territory, passed through the scullery and pulled open the heavy back door. Immediately the noise pressed down on her like an iron weight, her ears filled by its deep drumming. She thought it sounded like some monstrous traction-engine, and her eyes were pulled instinctively upwards to the source of the sound.

At first Elvira couldn't and wouldn't believe it. Her brain simply refused to accept the message transmitted to it by her eyes. She stared upwards, vacant-looking as a sleep-walker, at the great, silver cigar-shape that hung in the sky above the cottage, showing lights all down one side and throbbing like some gigantic and malevolent insect. Then suddenly it began to move, gliding slowly and gracefully towards the green. As it did so, a brightly-lit bluish object fell from it with a whistling shriek and there was an explosion that sent Elvira reeling against the scullery wall. Filled with panic in the darkness and mist, she felt that even the familiar backyard had become menacing. "Run! Run! Hide!" a voice screamed inside her head. "The Zeppelins are here! The Zeppelins!"

Elvira didn't think. She couldn't think. Instinctively she started to run for the Sanctuary, out of the front gate and along the road to Frissington St Peter. She felt no pain from the stones that bruised her bare feet, and was blind to the figures now running out of their houses and on to the green. "Run! Run!" the insistent voice screamed in her brain. Somewhere there was another explosion, then the shrill, piercing note of a police-whistle that went on and on. The church bells began to toll. Elvira ran on. Faster and faster. A few yards from the goosegrass path she had to stop, bent double with the sharp pain of a stitch in her side. Her breath came in deep sobs. Then she looked back and saw that the Zeppelin was following her, sailing towards her in an arrow-straight line, its terrible, whirring voice growing louder by the second. With a scream she flung herself across the ditch and started to stumble up the goosegrass path, twice slipping and falling flat before she eventually reached the coppice.

As she started through the trees she felt the coppice leap into life. Soon it was aquiver with the alarm-calls of roosting birds and the soft, frightened flurry of wings. Above the tree-tops, filling the dark vault with its terrible song, hung the Zeppelin like a monstrous bird of prey. "Hide! Hide!" Elvira sobbed under her breath, fighting in the nightmare darkness with branches that shot out to bar her way and brambles and briars which caught on her nightdress and tugged her back. She had almost reached the end of the coppice track and the edge of the meadow when she stumbled over a root and fell. So it was on hands and knees that she watched, frozen with terror, as the Zeppelin dropped its third and final bomb. Again she saw the bluish light hurtle earthwards and heard the peculiar, whistling shriek before the bang of the explosion which seemed, for a moment, to be inside her own skull. A great, black object somersaulted through the air and she realized in fascinated horror that it was the old apple tree. Almost immediately there was a noise like gigantic hailstones as a great shower of displaced earth and stones battered the Sanctuary, breaking its windows and scattering tiles from its roof. Then the engine noise in the sky grew fainter until it finally faded altogether. The birds quietened. And there was silence.

Elvira was shivering, shaking so hard that her teeth were chattering. She rose stiffly from her hands and knees, feeling icy cold and slightly sick. She started back the way she had come, beating her arms against her chest to bring some heat back into her body. It seemed that with every second step she trod on a jagged flint that dug into her foot and made her yelp. As she picked her way down the goosegrass path she saw the fire-engine pass by on its way to Frissington St Peter, and P.C. Appleby pedalling furiously behind it on his old bicycle. She was half crying with the cold and the pain of her bruised feet, when she finally arrived back at Frissington Angel green. Immediately a knot of people detached itself from the crowd gathered there and came hurrying to meet her. Rhoda, carrying Arthur, was at the head of them.

"Elvie!" she exclaimed, her voice crackly with relief. "Where in heaven's name have you been? I've been worried sick!"

"I went to hide . . . in the fields," Elvira admitted shamefacedly. "I'm sorry."

"And I should just think so!" Rhoda began when Mr Diaper intervened.

"Elvira Preston!" he exclaimed. "Reckon you're the only one in Frissington Angel that had any sense." He turned to Mr Honeyball who was standing beside him. "Suppose those Hun prisoners had broke out of the Camp and joined forces with them up in that Zep. Where would we all have been?" he demanded. Mr Honeyball shook his head despairingly.

"Exactly!" Mr Diaper went on. "Like fish in a net we'd have been. Standing here gawping on the green. But not our Elvira! Not her! She'd have given them the slip."

"Reckon so!" Mr Honeyball agreed with a chuckle. "Clever that lass is. Takes after her dad."

"I was scared to death. That's why I ran off," Elvira confessed to Rhoda ten minutes later when they were back indoors.

"So were we all," Rhoda told her. She had just taken Arthur up to bed and was lighting the lamp before making a pot of tea. It was still only fifteen minutes to midnight. Rhoda's dark eyes glowed sombrely in her white face as she looked at Elvira over the lamp.

"I thought it was the end of everything," she admitted. "When I came out and saw that great buzzing thing up there, I thought, So, old Mother Fisher was right after all! The spy's done for us all. We're going to be blown to smithereens."

"Was anyone hurt?" Elvira asked apprehensively.

"No," Rhoda replied, cheering up suddenly as she poked the sleeping fire into life. "All that noise and commotion and they didn't do a farthing's worth of damage! Two bombs dropped in the Windmill Field and the third up in the old brickfield, so P.C. Appleby reckons. And there's nothing up there but some old ruined place, they say."

Elvira crouched on the rug before the fire feeling the welcome heat on her hands and face. "When you think of what might have happened . . ." she began tremulously.

"Like blowing the whole of Frissington Angel sky-high," Rhoda finished, staring into the heart of the leaping flames. Suddenly she turned to look down on Elvira, a rather diffident expression on her normally resolute face. "Know what?" she said abruptly. "I'm beginning to believe in that golden angel, Elvie. The one Miss Kindness talks about. I'm beginning to think he must still be about here somewhere, keeping Frissington Angel from harm."

25

The Day After

It seemed that the whole of Frissington Angel was in a black mood the following morning. When Elvira ran across the green to the farm for the morning milk, she found Mr Mitchell angrily chasing off a bunch of scowling youngsters who had been searching for bomb fragments in the field behind the farm.

"Not that they were doing any harm," she remarked to Rhoda when she returned. "He only uses that field for his goats, grumpy old man!"

"You don't know anything about it, Elvie!" Rhoda retorted snappishly.

Darting a look at her stepmother's pale face and dark-ringed eyes, Elvira bit back the remonstrance that was on her lips. It was obvious that Rhoda was in one of her moods and Elvira had neither the energy nor the inclination to argue with her.

Arthur too was spoiling for a fight from the moment he opened his eyes, and by the time Elvira finally shoved him through Mrs Boniface's front door, she was feeling exhausted and quite prickly herself. It wasn't until Ethel Foster joined her at the foot of Factory Hill that Elvira's spirits rose a little. For Ethel was agog to hear about the Zeppelin and obviously envious that it had chosen Frissington Angel as its target and not Frissington St Peter.

"I didn't see hardly nothing!" she complained. "Even though Ma took us all out to the garden after the first bang. All I could see was a sort of pencil-thing in the sky ever so far away. What did it really look like, Elvie?"

By the time the Frissington Angel contingent arrived in the playground they had gathered quite an audience and the Zeppelin remained the main topic of conversation for the rest of the morning. Mr Christmas asked those who had actually seen the airship to write a composition on their impressions of it, while their less fortunate classmates wrestled with the intricacies of parsing. Then at the morning break Sophie Christmas came stalking self-importantly over to Elvira and her friends.

"Mrs Fisher thinks the Zep will come again," she announced dramatically. "She says it came here for a purpose. And since it didn't do any damage, it's bound to come back! Maybe with lots of others!"

"That's a lot of old squit!" George Pollitt called rudely from the playground wall. "My Grandpa reckons they were just getting rid of their bombs to make the Zep lighter for floating back across the sea."

"You wait and see then, Mr Know-All!" Sophie called, sticking her tongue out and tossing her red hair, before she ran off. "You'll soon find out who's right!"

In fact Sophie didn't have long to wait before she could assume her smuggest expression, because at the end of the dinner break, Sidney Spurgeon, who had been up to the harvest field to visit his dad, came clattering back into the schoolyard, his eyes popping with excitement.

"Old Appleby's just been up to the field to see my dad," he gasped, "an' you know what? He says someone was sending signals up to that old Zep last night! Someone up in Frissington Angel! He reckons they might even call in the military now."

Elvira gave a little shudder as she listened to this news. Standing in the bright noonday sunshine she felt again the icy terror that had seized her when she had first glimpsed the Zeppelin hovering above their backyard, and the idea that someone had deliberately lured it there to drop its deadly cargo now made her feel quite sick with fear.

"There now! What did I tell you! Mrs Fisher's been right all along. It's the spy that brought that Zep here. And he'll bring more if he's not caught." Sophie, her thin face flushed with triumph, pushed her way to the front of the throng and glared at her audience.

"Why don't you catch him then, if you're so clever, Sophie Christmas!" a voice sang out.

"Her! She couldn't catch a cold!" someone else jeered.

Elvira turned her back on the now bantering crowd and walked slowly over to the school building. How could they joke about something so horrible, she wondered? If they had been with her last night and seen that monstrous silver fish of a thing hanging up there in the sky . . . It wasn't so much the memory of the Zeppelin that was making her feel bad as the thought of that unseen enemy working in their midst and intent on destroying them all. What did he look like? She shut her eyes tight until she could almost envisage him. Mr Frissington Spy. Tall, dark, weasel-faced, with a hooked nose and cunning little eyes. Sliding along in the shadows as the Frissingtons slept . . .

The ringing of the school bell interrupted her thoughts and the headmaster appeared with a piece of important news for them. The chairman of the managers had just given Mr Christmas the date of the harvest holiday which was to begin the following Monday. An ear-splitting cheer went up from Standard 6 and it was quenched only by the headmaster thumping irately on his desk. Elvira shared wholeheartedly in her schoolmates' rejoicing. Not that she was particularly looking forward to four weeks' of caring for Arthur and keeping house, but it was better than school!

She waited eagerly that evening for Rhoda to come home so that she could tell her the news. But, as it happened, Rhoda had her own piece of news to impart. And the implications behind it, as far as Elvira was concerned, were to make an ordinary event like a holiday seem relatively unimportant.

26

A Letter to Clarry

"Now, maybe I shouldn't be telling you," Rhoda said in a low voice, her eyes glowing as she sat across from Elvira nursing Arthur on her lap. "Only this airman came into the factory today to have a look at the new plane we're making and he must have heard us talking about our Zep. For he came walking over after a bit and said, 'I believe that was the LZ 71 that paid you a visit last night. Did you know we'd brought it down in the sea?' "

"They didn't! Did they really?" Elvira exclaimed.

Rhoda nodded and Elvira knew from her face that there was more to come. "We asked him if the crew had all been drowned," she continued. "But he said no. That they all got ashore and surrendered. And that when they were interrogated they told everything about their raid, including how they'd bombed a place they thought at first was Ipswich, but it turned out to be just a tiny village."

"Frissington Angel?" Elvira queried.

"Yes," Rhoda replied, then stopped to take a breath, because she was coming to the most important part of her story. "The airman said he shouldn't really tell us the next bit," she continued, "only he didn't see any harm in it as he reckoned we'd be hearing about it soon, anyway."

"Go on then!" Elvira urged.

"It's just that there was someone in Frissington Angel signalling to that Zep, Elvie!"

"Oh, I know that . . ." Elvira began, but Rhoda added, "Signalling German words they were. In morse. With a powerful electric torch. What do you think of that?"

In the silence that followed, the ticking of the clock and the burbling of the potato pot sounded abnormally loud. Finally Elvira asked slowly, "Did the airman tell you what the signals said?"

"Yes, he did," Rhoda told her eagerly. "Apparently the first thing the Zep crew saw was the word 'here' being signalled over and over again, though in German, as I said. They were lost at that point and had come down low to try to get their bearings. When they saw the signal they were sure they were over some important target."

"So then they dropped their bombs," Elvira put in.

"No. Not directly," Rhoda replied "because then the signaller started giving directions. First they were told 'left'. Then it changed to 'right' after they'd dropped the first bomb. The Zep captain still thought they were on the outskirts of Ipswich until they dropped a flare and saw open country all around."

"So someone really did want Frissington Angel bombed?" Elvira muttered.

"Some Hun agent that's hidden up in the district," Rhoda rejoined. "That's what we think at the factory, anyway. We reckon he's out to get us aeroplane workers and halt production just when we're busy with this new plane."

Elvira swallowed and licked her lips because her mouth had suddenly gone very dry. "I don't suppose it could have been one of those German prisoners?" she finally brought out.

"No, Elvie. I shouldn't think that's likely," Rhoda replied, lowering little Arthur to the floor and standing up to prod the potatoes with a long fork. "None of them are likely to be wandering around the countryside after dark, are they? I mean how could they get over that great, high wall for a start? And I shouldn't think they'd allow them to have electric torches," she finished with a chuckle.

"Why are they so sure the signaller used an electric torch?" Elvira asked, as she spread the teacloth over the table. "It

140

might have been a storm-lantern."

"Well that's what the Zep captain said," Rhoda told her, as she opened the staircase door to go up to her room and change. "And I should think he's had plenty of experience with signals. So he ought to know what he's talking about."

To begin with it was just the vaguest suspicion which touched Elvira every so often and made her feel uncomfortable. It wasn't until darkness fell and the terror of the previous night's raid returned vividly to her mind that her doubts really began to crowd in on her and refused to let her fall asleep. Could it have been Bill who had signalled to the Zeppelin? Was it possible that someone she looked on as a trusted friend could have betrayed her? "No, no, no!" her heart protested vehemently. But her head responded with arguments that became more and more convincing. Wasn't it just too much of a coincidence, for example, that Bill should have asked for an electric torch last week? And what about the musical box he'd given her, bought in Frankfurt where the field-glasses had come from? Had he laid his plans from the very first moment of his meeting Clarry and her up in the Sanctuary? Had he seen them as easy targets, youngsters who could be taken in by soft talk and a few kind words? And now he was planning to escape to Germany with her help, and heaven knows what information he might be taking with him! Things he had overheard while passing knots of gossiping villagers. Careless talk by guards, who didn't know he spoke English fluently. Even she might have given him bits of information about the aeroplane factory without realizing it.

All next day the black cloud of fear and suspicion hung over Elvira's head. And a new notion had come to torment her, too. If Bill were what she feared then she, Elvira, had been largely responsible for bringing the Zeppelin to Frissington Angel. If anyone had been killed she would have been a murderess. It was too awful to bear on her own. So when Mr Christmas told them in the afternoon that they could use what was left of their

English exercise books in any way they liked, she decided immediately to write to Clarry. It was such a relief to bring her problem out into the open that she had soon filled a page, her left arm carefully protecting her writing from inquisitive eyes. She was three-quarters of the way down the second page and had just explained to Clarry that she had arranged a midnight rendezvous with Bill on Thursday, when the headmaster rang the bell for afternoon break. Seeing Flora Crack beckoning to her from the doorway, Elvira closed her exercise book and took the precaution of placing her pencil box on top of it to anchor it down. But as she hurried down the passageway to join Flora, she was quite unaware that Sophie Christmas had been watching her curiously and was now making her way across the classroom towards Elvira's desk.

Elvira begged an envelope and a stamp from Rhoda and ran down to Frissington St Peter at half-past-seven that night to post her letter to Clarry. Not that she could possibly receive any answer from him before her midnight meeting with Bill, but it had helped just to tell him about her dilemma. She was on her way home and passing Mrs Boniface's, when she spied Mrs Honeyball hurrying in at their gate to have a chat with Rhoda. A wave of despondency swept over her. She could imagine what all the talk would be about this evening. Zeppelins and bombs and spies. Suddenly she couldn't bear to hear another syllable on the subject. Not on a beautiful summer evening like this. Darting over to the other side of the green, she hurried past a crowd of 'little 'uns', who were playing chases and made her way to the green, rustling solitude of the overgrown churchyard. Sitting on the old seat, she remembered again how dreadful she had been feeling the last time she'd come here, just after they'd heard about Dad going missing. Now she looked down on the ramshackle little village and all at once she realized just how dearly she loved the place. Every sagging roof and crumbling wall. Every tree. Every blade of grass. How dare those hateful Huns try to destroy it! How dare they!

"Elvie!" The whispered summons came from behind her, and Elvira swung round and gave a little gasp as she stared disbelievingly at the church porch. Bill was standing in the shadow beckoning to her! She rose reluctantly, wishing in her heart that she could turn and run. At the same time though, she wanted desperately to tell him that she was opting out of their Thursday rendezvous, that she wanted no more to do with him. It would be such a relief to make her position quite clear — to show the German that he couldn't dupe her any longer.

"Elvie! What a surprise!" Bill's thin face lit up. "The rector asked if I'd like to come this evening to play the organ and I thought I would. For one last time, you know. But I never thought to see you here."

Elvira stood dumbly at the entrance to the porch, her eyes fixed on the young man as though she were willing him to read her mind.

"The rector is in the vestry," Bill whispered. "I don't expect he would mind if he saw us talking, but . . ." His voice died abruptly as he noticed Elvira's expression. He was silent for a moment, then he asked slowly, "Whatever is the matter, Elvie? Why are you looking at me like that?"

Staring at Bill's anxious face and at his perturbed blue eyes, Elvira found herself unable to think or speak coherently. She felt hot and flustered and ready to burst into tears. Eventually she blurted out a string of disconnected phrases. "Someone signalling to the Zep . . . an electric torch . . . in German . . . the Frissington spy . . . trying to kill Rhoda and her workmates . . . thinking about it for two days . . . now I know . . ."

It was some time before Bill's voice broke the silence that fell between them, and when it did it was tight and hurt and shook a little. "And you think it was me!" he said, adding, "Oh, Elvie! Elvie! How could you! I thought we were such friends!"

As soon as Elvira plucked up the courage to look Bill straight in the eye she knew that her suspicions had been groundless. His was one of those open faces like her dad's, that could hide nothing, and at that moment he was looking as though he had been punched hard on the chin by his best mate. He couldn't be pretending: it wasn't possible!

"I'm sorry, Bill! Of course it wasn't you! I'm really sorry!" she managed to say before she turned her head away to blink back tears of relief.

Bill's hand fell comfortingly on her shoulder. "It's all right, Elvie," he said softly. "It's not your fault. It's the poison of war. It affects us all at times. It's impossible to escape it."

She nodded to show she understood, then felt her hair tweaked playfully. "See you tomorrow then. As arranged," Bill whispered, before vanishing into the church and closing the door quietly behind him.

As Elvira ran down the path towards the churchyard gate the deep, golden voice of the organ floated out into the pink and saffron evening sky, banishing the memory of the malevolent airship that had hung over the Frissingtons two nights before.

27

The Rendezvous

From the moment Mr Christmas printed the date Thursday, August 8th, across the top of the blackboard the following morning, Elvira began to feel peculiar. She wasn't exactly sick, but every now and again butterflies would flutter wildly in her stomach, and then she would experience the sinking sensation she usually associated with visits to the travelling dentist. As the time for the rendezvous with Bill drew nearer, the more ominous it seemed. Helping an enemy prisoner escape! As she sucked her pencil for inspiration during the arithmetic lesson, her eyes roamed around the class and she thought how no one else in the room would help a German prisoner run away! No one in the whole of Suffolk probably! And if anyone in the Frissingtons guessed what she was going to do tonight . . .

But Mr Christmas's ruler snapping down on her desk put an end to her musings and she started so violently that she broke her pencil and was made to stand in the corner for fifteen minutes with her face to the wall.

At dinner break Sophie Christmas came sidling along to where Elvira and Lizzie Pitt were sitting in the shadow of the big oak tree. "Supposing you were granted a wish, Elvira Preston. What would it be?" she asked, pirouetting around on one foot.

"To have my dad back, of course," Elvira said inwardly. But she had no intention of baring her soul to Sophie Christmas, so she only shrugged and stared beyond Sophie across the playground.

"I know what I would wish for," Sophie announced, looking down at the two girls with an odd little simper. "I would wish that I could trap the Frissington spy . . . So there!" And with a toss of her red head she darted away.

"She's barmy!" Lizzie Pitt exclaimed, finishing off her bread and cheese with a gulp. "She's been gawping at you all morning, Elvie. Haven't you noticed?"

Elvira shook her head, only half listening. She was wondering whether there would be a moon that night or whether she ought to risk sneaking the storm-lantern from the scullery cupboard and hiding it in her room.

"And she's a sly one, too," Lizzie was going on, following Sophie's progress with narrowing eyes. "Isn't she, Elvie? Isn't she sly?" She nudged Elvie, jolting her out of her reverie.

"Oh, who cares!" sighed Elvira, standing up and dusting down her skirt. "Only one more day of school, then we don't need to look at any Christmases for weeks and weeks."

"There she goes again!" Lizzie exclaimed. "Gawping across the yard at you, as though you'd grown horns or something. Whatever's come over the gel?"

But Elvira was lost in her own thoughts and didn't hear.

"Aren't you going to make us any supper then, Elvie?" Rhoda

asked, looking up from her mending. Elvira glanced at the clock and saw that it was a quarter-to-ten. "You hadn't an idea what the time was, had you?" Rhoda went on, shaking her head despairingly. "You're just like your dad! Get your nose stuck in a book and you might as well be unconscious."

Elvira didn't contradict her stepmother, but in fact she hadn't been reading at all. Ever since Arthur had been put to bed she had been sitting on the couch beneath the window staring unseeingly at page forty-two of *Christy's Old Organ* and checking over in her mind all the preparations for her rendezvous with Bill. As soon as she had arrived home from school and had settled Arthur on the back-doorstep with his milk and cake, she had flown upstairs to Rhoda's room and opened the big mahogany wardrobe where her father's clothes were hanging. With fingers that trembled she had taken out his best, cord trousers, his black waistcoat, a checked shirt and his second best jacket. Then standing on tiptoe, she had pulled down a grey cap and a red neckerchief. She had rolled the lot into a sausage-shaped bundle and darted over to her own room and shoved it under the mattress at the bottom of her bed. She had decided against taking the storm-lantern since, even if the night did turn out cloudy, she felt she was hardly likely to lose her way. And to carry a light was to run the risk of being spotted by some wakeful villager. Now all she had to do, she reflected as she set about making the cocoa, was to keep awake until half-past-eleven, and to slip out of the house without disturbing Arthur or Rhoda.

"You look real tired tonight, Elvie," Rhoda remarked suddenly. "You make your cocoa good and strong. It'll help you to sleep."

Her words sent a stab of apprehension through Elvira and she hurriedly poured half of the milk from the pan back into the jug. "Don't feel much like cocoa tonight," she said. "Think I'll have a cup of tea instead."

"Talk about Miss Contrary!" Rhoda exclaimed, tight-lipped. Elvira could see she had annoyed her by the way her needle began to flash in and out of the sock she was mending.

146

Rhoda was still huffy when they both went to bed half an hour later, and having peeped into Elvira's room to see that Arthur was asleep, she whispered the briefest of good-nights to her stepdaughter before closing her own bedroom door.

And that's all to the good, Elvira thought, as she slipped, fully clothed under the counterpane and felt the bundle of her father's clothes beneath her feet. She had left the door slightly ajar so that she could listen to the chimes of the clock from the living-room below and now she heard the double note that told her it was half-past-ten. The realization that a whole hour's wait lay ahead of her was daunting at first, for she daren't light the candle to read in case she wakened Arthur. Then she remembered how her dad had taught her to occupy herself if she had any waiting to do.

"Reciting," he would declare. "It's the best time-passer there is. Out loud or inside your head. It doesn't matter. Just work through all the poems you've ever known."

She started with the saddest one she knew. One that Dad had taught her himself about a little girl called Mary who was gleaning in a cornfield and who was asked why she didn't rest under the tree with the others. Her answer always brought tears to Elvira's eyes.

Oh, no! For my mother lies ill in her bed,
Too feeble to spin or to knit;
And my poor little brothers are crying for bread,
And yet we can't give them a bit.

Tonight Elvira felt even worse about poor Mary and her family because she was reminded of Bill's sister, Siggi, who might well be just as hungry. She recited the tribulations of little Mary once more before moving on to happier subjects such as the Old Woman of Lynn, 'whose nose very near touched her chin,' and the Old Woman named Towl, 'who went out to sea with her owl'. She was about to start on 'Meg Merrilies' when the clock downstairs began to chime eleven and almost immediately Arthur sat upright in his cot.

Elvira lay still hardly daring to breathe, hoping against hope that the little boy would lie down again and fall asleep. But Arthur gave an ominous whimper that had Elvira on her feet and across the room in a second.

"Artie want a drink!" he whined crossly, and Elvira darted over to the covered jug and cup on the washstand. She pulled back the window curtain so that the room was silvered with moonlight.

"There now!" she whispered soothingly when Arthur had sipped at the water, "Artie lie down again and Elvie'll tell him a story."

" 'Bout the Billy-Goats Gruff!" he stipulated fiercely, and she launched into the story without delay.

But Elvira had exhausted her entire stock of fairy-tales and it was half-past-eleven before Arthur was properly asleep again.

She waited motionless for five minutes, listening to the little boy's regular breathing before she dared to lift her mattress and pull out the roll of clothing. Then she picked up her boots, and with the clothes under her arm she sidled through the open door and tiptoed downstairs. Once she was in the scullery she slipped on her boots and sat on the floor to lace them up. She had just tied the laces of the right one when a short, sharp creak on the staircase set her scalp prickling. She froze for a moment but could hear nothing except the hammer-beats of her own heart. Just the old boards turning in their sleep, she told herself finally. That was how her dad had always described the mysterious noises the house made at night. She got carefully to her feet, opened the scullery door and slipped out into the warm night.

A soft little breeze fanned Elvira's flushed cheeks and every now and again it puffed the moon into hiding behind a thistle-down cloud. She didn't mind the dark patches because they hid the bats that were zig-zagging back and forth across the track just above her head. From behind Mitchells' farmhouse a screech-owl kept calling plaintively. Proper eerie this is, she thought as she broke into a trot, and she couldn't help wishing once again that Clarry was by her side. He'd have enjoyed it, she reflected. It's every bit as exciting as what those children of the New Forest did.

As she stopped for a moment to catch her breath, her elation vanished and cold little fingers of fear crept up her spine. Something had moved in the darkness behind her. She knew it, though she wasn't sure what or where. It could have been the scrape of a footstep or the swish of clothing. She stood like a statue, her father's clothes pressed hard against her chest, waiting for the moon to slide out from behind a cloud. Despite the warmth of the night, her teeth began to chatter. Then from the dry ditch just beside her came a single, sharp squeal and a white shape sprang out to dive by Elvira's legs. Her breath hissed out in blessed relief. It was only Kitty, Mrs Boniface's cat, hunting a mouse for her supper!

Elvira hurried on, cross with herself for panicking. It's that horrid spy! she thought. Can't help thinking about him when you're out in the dark. Nasty, sneaky old snake! Wish they'd catch him! Then once more, just after she had jumped the ditch and crawled through the fence on to the goosegrass path, she stopped short imagining she heard another sound behind her. But when she saw the tall, full heads of the wheat swinging gently in the breeze, tap-tapping together, she relaxed again. "Scared of the wind! Whatever next!" she scolded herself in a whisper, as she turned her eyes determinedly ahead and started to hurry up the long path. The sound she heard as she approached the entrance to the coppice was no trick of her imagination, though. It was Bill calling to her in a low voice to warn her that he was standing in the trees awaiting her arrival, one hand carefully shading the torch she had given him.

"I thought you might find it difficult picking your way through the trees," he whispered as he gripped her welcomingly by the shoulder.

Elvira, smiling a little nervously, handed the German the bundle of clothing. Her mission was over, she thought. Now she had only to say her farewells to her friend and she could hurry back to Frissington green. But Bill was looking at her anxiously.

"I have to ask one more favour of you, Elvie," he said finally. "I hate to do it, because it may be dangerous for you. But if you could keep my uniform hidden for a few days, it would give me a better chance of getting away. They may think I'm still wearing it, you see . . ."

Elvira nodded unhesitatingly. She knew where she could hide Bill's uniform. Under the mattress where she had hidden her dad's clothes. Rhoda would never look there. Not until the Christmas cleaning anyway. And by that time . . .

"Thank you. Thank you," Bill was saying, his voice a little wobbly now as he turned to guide her with his torch through the dark, silent ranks of trees. When they were halfway along the path a roosting bird suddenly flew up behind them with a cry of alarm and a great beating of wings. Bill wheeled round with a sharp intake of breath.

"It's all right," Elvira assured him. "It's only a woodpigeon. The torchlight must have scared it."

Bill smiled, but the hand that was holding the torch was trembling visibly. How scared he must be, Elvira thought as he walked on again. Poor Bill! If it hadn't been for Siggi he'd probably have stopped quite happily in Frissington until the War was over.

When they finally came out of the coppice on to the meadow Bill put a warning hand on Elvira's arm. "You must be careful here," he told her. "The bomb did a lot of damage. As well as uprooting the apple tree it blew out the concrete plug from the well. There are lumps of it scattered all over. And near the house there are bits of glass from the windows."

Elvira looked across at the Sanctuary and at the bald patches on its roof clearly visible in the moonlight. "Is the house safe?" she asked apprehensively.

"I think so," Bill told her. "Safe enough for me to use as a changing-room anyway. Will you be all right outside here, if I take the torch? I have to collect my things from the cupboard."

"I'll be fine," Elvira assured him.

Nevertheless, after Bill had gone she couldn't help glancing uneasily at the black depths of the coppice behind her and straining her ears to identify the minute sounds that came from it: squeaks and rustlings and the whisperings of leaves. If she stared too hard her eyes began to see human shapes in the inanimate shadows and she had to scare these ghosts away by blinking rapidly. Finally she felt she needed a change of scene and she picked her way cautiously round to the back of the house to see what damage the bomb had wreaked there. In fact there wasn't much. A stable roof had fallen in. And Clarry's woodpile, of which he had been so proud, was scattered in all directions. She was staring at the spot where the pile had once stood, remembering that far off evening when Clarry had started building it. Then a short, sharp scream from the front of the Sanctuary sent her heart into her mouth.

"Those dratted owls!" she exclaimed viciously, when she had recovered from her fright. "Wish I'd a gun with me! I'd stop their screeching!"

But seeing the remnants of the woodpile had reminded Elvira of the well. It was unblocked now, Bill had said. Just what she and Clarry had wanted! And now it was too late. She decided to go back round to the front of the house and have a look at it. After all she might never come up to the Sanctuary again now that both Clarry and Bill were gone. She picked her way carefully through the grass, avoiding the jagged lumps of concrete that were strewn about. The moon was shining clearly now and as Elvira drew near to the well, she could see the top rungs of a narrow iron ladder that had been stapled to the inside of the circular brick wall and which disappeared down into the depths.

That must have been for when they cleared it out, she reflected. I wonder if it's dried up now or if there's still water down there. She moved closer and as she did so, she saw Bill coming out of the house and crossing towards her. She was craning her neck over the low, crumbling wall of the well, not daring to lean on it. But she could see nothing. Only inky blackness.

"Here," Bill whispered, coming up to her. "Use your father's torch. I need a second to tie my bundle more securely."

"Thanks." Elvira took the torch, and as she did so, she scrutinized Bill sharply. "That's fine," she assured him at last. "You look just like Dad and his friends. No one will guess the clothes aren't yours."

She turned back to the well as Bill knelt to retie the neckerchief in which he was carrying his possessions. The young man didn't see Elvira suddenly freeze or the expression of mingled horror and incredulity that slipped over her face. He heard the weird, little noise that she made, though. A choked scream that wavered into a wail of appalled despair. And he sprang in perturbation to his feet.

"Elvie! What is it? What's wrong?" he demanded, forgetting in his fear to keep his voice low.

Elvira, standing in the moonlight, like some pale, distraught ghost, pointed silently at first down into the well behind her. Finally, with an immense effort, she managed to speak.

"It's Artie! My little brother, Bill! Down there in the well!" Her voice began to rise hysterically. "He must have followed me like he did before . . . I thought I heard someone behind me. And that scream! It wasn't the owl! It was him falling! My little brother! I must get to him, Bill! I must!"

"Elvie! What is this? What are you saying?" Bill, aghast, started forward. But even as he did so, Elvira moved. Dropping the torch, she suddenly swung herself over the side of the well and on to the iron ladder.

"Elvie! No! What are you doing? Stop!" Bill's desperate command came too late. There was a grinding noise as the rusted staples wrenched themselves loose from the bricks, and Elvira felt herself swing outwards until her back bumped hard against the wall on the opposite side.

"Keep still! Very still, Elvie!" Bill's voice called urgently from above her head and almost immediately the ladder ceased to sway. "I am holding the top of the ladder," he went on, his voice now quite calm and steady. "And I am going to shine the torch down, so don't look up or you may be dazzled."

Elvira kept as still as was possible for she was trembling all over with shock and fright, sandwiched as she was between the cold brick of the wall and the iron bars of the ladder, and hardly daring to breathe.

A moment later the blackness was illuminated by the powerful beam of the torch, and she could see that just beneath the level of her feet the brick wall gave place to smooth, moss-covered wood. And she forced herself to look down – down, to the very bottom of the well where the little boy in the white nightgown sprawled silent and unmoving.

28

Discovered!

"Elvie! . . . Elvie!" Bill's insistent voice finally penetrated Elvira's numbed brain. She tore her eyes from the appalling sight beneath to ask faintly. "What? What is it?"

"There are people coming!" Bill told her. "Lots of people coming through the coppice!" His voice wobbled with apprehension, but at the same time he sounded relieved. "They are carrying lights," he went on. "When they come out on to the meadow, I'll shine the torch towards them so that they can see where we are."

Stunned as she was by shock and grief at the tragedy that had overtaken her, Elvira was still sufficiently aware to grasp the implications behind Bill's words.

"No!" she protested looking up to where Bill stood by the ladder. "Run, Bill! Now! While you still have a chance . . . I'll shout for help. They're bound to hear me."

"No. I cannot leave you until I know you are safe," Bill's voice came down to her, soft but decisive. "And until I hear about the child."

Elvira looked down again to where Artie lay, so silent, so motionless. If only she could get to him to find out how badly he was hurt! But she was terrified to move now in case the rusting ladder fell to bits or the crumbling brickwork at her back began to disintegrate. Her head was beginning to swim a little when Bill called out sharply, "Here they come!" and swung the torch up so that she was plunged into blackness. She clung grimly to the ladder's rungs, hardly aware that the rough corroded iron was scraping the skin from her palms. She could hear voices now raised in excitement and anger. A man shouted, "Stop where you are! No tricks now!" and she heard Bill try to explain what had happened, before pandemonium erupted.

A voice, unmistakably Sophie Christmas's, was calling shrilly, "I told you so! Didn't I tell you so! I read it all in her letter in her exercise book!" Elvira caught the headmaster's gruff, "Well done, child!" before the angry buzz above her head began to swell in volume and she was dazzled by the light of at least a dozen torches and lamps flooding down into the well.

"There she is! The little traitor!" Elvira immediately recognized the strident tones as Mrs Fisher's.

Then Rhoda's voice, hoarse with indignation, called out, "You mind your tongue, Mrs Fisher! That's my gel you're miscalling!"

Elvira closed her eyes tightly as the babble increased to a crescendo. It was like a horrible dream. Perhaps it was a bad dream, she thought for a moment. Perhaps she would wake up and be back in her room with Artie safe in his cot beside her. But then directly above her head, the Reverend Robson-Turner called for silence in a voice like thunder. Elvira had never heard him so angry.

"You fools!" he fumed. "Don't you realize what danger young Elvira's in down there? And that there's apparently some other child at the bottom of the well?"

"Another child?" Mrs Groom's plaintive voice broke the shocked silence that had followed the rector's statement.

"That's what the German lad's been trying to tell you," the rector continued angrily. "Elvira thought it was her little brother who had followed her. She was trying to get down to him."

"More like trying to hide when she saw us coming," Mrs Fisher put in spitefully, and Rhoda retorted with a vicious, "Shut your mouth, you old witch!" She then called out loudly, "Elvie, love! Artie's safe at home with old Mrs Boniface. So don't you be imagining things and scaring yourself!"

Relief at Rhoda's words surged through Elvira like a warm, life-giving tide, then as suddenly ebbed away, leaving her weak and shaking. "I want to come up!" she wailed. "Can't you get me up? I feel ever so funny!"

"Hold on a moment, Elvie, gel!" P.C. Appleby was talking to her now, trying not very successfully to conceal his alarm. "I've sent a lad to the Old Rectory for a rope," he called down, "and I reckon I can see him right now coming back through the trees. So don't you go fainting or anything silly like that! D'you hear?"

"Yes," she muttered, but she was already feeling cold and sweaty and there was an ominous ringing in her ears.

"Wiggle your toes, Elvie! As hard as you can! Right now! And keep wiggling them. You won't faint then!" Bill's voice dropped down to her like a lifeline, calm and authoritative. She obeyed him and almost immediately felt the faintness recede.

"Thanks, Bill!" she called loyally. "It's worked. I'm all right now!"

"Listen to her! Talking to the Hun as though he were her best friend," Mrs Fisher was starting when the boy arrived with the rope and P.C. Appleby began directing the rescue operation.

It was a simple manoeuvre. They made a lasso and dropped it over her and all Elvira had to do was pull her arms through and hold the loop round her waist until they pulled it tight.

"Now just start to climb the ladder, my dear," P.C. Appleby instructed her. "Even if a rung goes now you'll be quite safe on the rope."

She was just about to start her ascent when Mr Spurgeon, who was helping the policeman, let out an exclamation. He had directed the beam of his torch to one side to avoid shining it in Elvira's eyes and had inadvertently fixed it on the small, white-robed figure at the bottom of the well.

"Darn! The gel was right! Gave me a proper turn and all!" he exploded. "But that's never flesh and blood. It's stone! Some sort of statue covered with a sheet . . . See, Henry?" The elderly labourer at his elbow was agreeing volubly when P.C. Appleby interrupted them impatiently. An old statue could wait, he informed them. Elvira Preston couldn't. So would they please keep their lights steady!

Elvira began to climb, her legs and arms mechanically performing the movements required of them. Inwardly though she felt lost in a fog of conflicting emotions. The revelation that it wasn't Artie lying at the bottom of the well, that it wasn't a living thing at all had removed the worst horror from the nightmare into which she had been plunged. But there were other ugly shapes sliding in to take its place. There was the knowledge that through her stupidity and carelessness, Bill's chances of escape had been destroyed. And almost as bad was the realization that when she reached the top of the ladder she would face the Frissington neighbours whom she had known all her life, no longer as a friend, but as an enemy. A traitor. "Oh, Dad! If only you were here!" she whispered with an anguished little sob. For Dad's strong, loving arms would have encircled her no matter what she had done. That was the one thing in the world that she was sure of.

It was Rhoda's arms that were waiting to receive Elvira when P.C. Appleby lifted her over the parapet of the well. Rhoda had obviously dressed in a hurry, pulling on her factory uniform over her nightdress, her unbrushed hair standing out in a frizzy halo around her pale face. She gave Elvira a quick, tight hug, then said in a loud voice.

"Right, Elvie, my gel! It's bed for you! You're as white as a sheet. Let's be going!"

"Not so fast! Not so fast, Mrs Preston!" It was Mrs Fisher's voice of course, vibrating with suppressed rage.

Reluctantly Elvira raised her head, and for the first time looked at her welcoming committee. There were people there from both the Frissingtons, about forty in all, staring at her with hard, solemn faces. She was to learn later that Mrs Fisher and Mr Christmas had organized the party in order to trap Bill and her at their rendezvous. Watchers had been posted between the Prestons' cottage and the Sanctuary. P.C. Appleby had been informed only when it was certain that Elvira was keeping her appointment with the German. The police constable in his turn had thought it advisable to tell the rector what was happening, and the Reverend Robson-Turner had rushed up to Frissington Angel to rouse Rhoda. For a moment Elvira was only aware of the circle of hostile faces. Then she saw Bill in her dad's clothes standing dejectedly to one side, handcuffed, with the rector's hand placed comfortingly on his shoulder, and Sophie Christmas at the very front of the group, eyes glittering with triumph, standing between her grandfather and Mrs Fisher.

The shopkeeper stepped forward now, looking to Elvira like some malevolent toad. "This girl is wicked!" she declaimed, her thick neck swelling as her voice rose. "She has put all our lives in danger. A little snake-in-the-grass helping the Huns! Helping the devil over there, the Frissington Spy, to bring the Zeppelins to bomb us!" She pointed a trembling finger towards Bill, then spat, wiping her podgy hand across her mouth.

Elvira felt Rhoda's arm tighten around her shoulders, and at the same time her courage returned. What right had Mrs Fisher to say things like that about her! And about Bill! She knew suddenly that she had to make her own voice heard, no matter what these people thought of her.

"Bill's not a spy!" she shouted in a high, quavering voice that sounded strange even in her own ears. "He's good and kind. As kind as my dad!" She glanced towards the young German just as the rector raised his lamp a little, so she caught the smile that illuminated Bill's drawn face for a moment. "Bill

157

had to escape to look for his young sister," she went on. "She's an orphan. And she might be ill and starving. That's why I gave Bill Dad's clothes and the things from his parcel. That's why I wanted to help him escape . . . And I'd help him again if I could!" she finished defiantly. "So there!"

A sound like 'Bravo!' came from the Reverend Robson-Turner. But Mr Christmas gave an audible gasp of disbelieving horror while a menacing murmur went up from the others. Mrs Fisher completely lost her head and bore down on Elvira screaming, "Evil! Evil! Evil!" until a sharp slap from the flat of Rhoda's right hand silenced her hysterical outburst. Rhoda walked forward slowly then straightened her shoulders and looked round the shadowy faces gathered about her. In other circumstances she would have presented a comic figure – her flannel nightgown gathered into unbecoming bulges under her uniform trousers, and her great frizz of hair. As it was, Elvira thought she had never looked more noble.

"Now look here, friends," she began in a level voice, but one that carried clearly across the meadow. "I want to hear no more about my Elvie being 'wicked' or 'evil'. She's a good girl. I should know. I live with her. She couldn't be better to Artie. And she was an angel to me when I was so ill with the influenza. If Elvie helped that young man over there, it was out of the goodness of her heart because she has a good and loving heart. Just like her dad. So you let her be! All of you!" she finished fiercely.

A lump had come into Elvira's throat and hot tears were prickling behind her eyes as Rhoda came back to her. But Mrs Fisher hadn't finished yet.

"Out of the goodness of her heart was it that she gave that Hun the torch?" she demanded. "So's he could climb up Mitchells' windmill and signal to his friends in the Zeppelin? You call that goodness? You . . ."

But P.C. Appleby who had been standing by the well had stepped forward, his hand upraised for silence, and the shop-keeper shut her mouth obediently.

"Mrs Fisher," the policeman said slowly, "how did you

know those signals were made from the windmill?"

The quiet that followed was almost palpable. No one stirred or coughed. There wasn't a rustle from the coppice. It seemed to Elvira as though the whole world had stopped breathing.

"Well, everyone knew that," the woman replied finally, her words falling into the deep pool of silence like pebbles.

"Oh, no! . . . No, no, no!" P.C. Appleby removed his helmet and wiped his brow. "No one knew that, Mrs Fisher. Except the Zep crew, the military authorities, myself and the spy, of course. It was being kept very dark, you see. So's we could trap the spy if he tried signalling from there again."

Everyone was staring silently at Mrs Fisher now, moving forward in their semi-circle, little by little, as though mesmerized. It was like some magical ceremony, Elvira thought, watching wide-eyed as the bobbing lamps and torches moved closer and closer together. The moon which had been hidden for the best part of half an hour suddenly appeared from behind a cloud, lighting Mrs Fisher's white, guilty face. The shopkeeper seemed to deflate even as Elvira watched. Her mouth sagged open and her black, button eyes became round with apprehension. Then, quite unexpectedly, she made a break for it, diving between Bill and the rector and moving with surprising speed across the meadow towards the coppice.

But someone else was faster. Sophie Christmas, like a voracious whippet after its prey, shot off in Mrs Fisher's wake and managed to grab the woman's apron strings, holding on grimly until P.C. Appleby and Mr Spurgeon came running to take charge of the sobbing fugitive.

"Well held! Well held, indeed!" Mr Christmas congratulated his returning grand-daughter. There were no supporting cheers from the crowd, though. The villagers stood silent for a moment, then began to drift away in knots towards the coppice. P.C. Appleby agreed to the rector escorting Bill back to the Camp while he took charge of Mrs Fisher. Rhoda put her arm around Elvira's shoulders again as they watched the group disperse.

"Well, fancy that!" she breathed. "Old Mother Fisher, the

Frissington Spy. I'd never have believed it! Doesn't seem to make sense somehow." Then she glanced down at her step-daughter and shook her head. "You look proper worn out after your adventures. And no wonder!" she exclaimed. "Let's get home, and tuck you into bed."

But Elvira wasn't quite ready to go yet. She turned round to face the Sanctuary. "Rhoda," she said hesitantly. "There's something you ought to know. I was going to run away from you and Artie and hide up in there until Dad came home."

Rhoda said nothing, just nodded slowly and stood looking sadly at the moonlit, tumbledown house.

"You see, I thought you didn't care about me," Elvira went on with a rush. "Not like you care about Artie and Dad, I mean. Then tonight when you stood up for me like that . . . just like Dad would have done . . . and said all those things . . ." Her voice cracked suddenly and broke off.

They were quite alone in the meadow now. Rhoda turned to face Elvira, putting a hand on each of her shoulders.

"Elvie," she said softly. "You're my daughter and I love you just as much as I love Artie. Maybe I don't show it. I'm not one of those kissing and cuddling folk. But I love you all the same. I would never have managed without you these past few months. You've been a real comfort to me and I know you always will be." As they set off for home with Rhoda holding the storm-lantern high to light them through the coppice, Elvira tugged gently at her stepmother's arm.

"If you don't mind, Rhoda," she said, "I think I'd like to start calling you 'Mam' instead of 'Rhoda'."

"That would make me proud and very happy," Rhoda said quietly, as they walked on.

Revelations

Elvira didn't go to school the following day because Rhoda said they couldn't expect old Mrs Boniface to take Arthur after sitting up waiting for them until half-past-one that morning.

"Anyway, it is the last day of term and you don't look fit to go. You look proper peaky and tired," Rhoda remarked, as she and Elvira breakfasted together.

"I don't feel up to facing them all yet, anyway," Elvira admitted, frowning down into her cup. When she looked up at Rhoda, her dark eyes were anxious. "Do you think they'll hate me? For helping a German?" she asked a little shakily.

" 'Course they won't!" Rhoda declared as she rose from the table and prepared to leave for work. "It'll be Old Mother Fisher, the Frissington Spy, they'll be talking about today! They'll have forgotten all about you, Elvie."

And sure enough, when Mrs Honeyball came rapping excitedly at the back door at ten o'clock that morning, it was to tell Elvira the latest developments in the Fisher drama.

"It's like one of those 'venture stories! It truly is, Elvie!" she exclaimed, stepping over Arthur's wheelbarrow and coming in to perch on the arm of the sofa. "It comes out now that Mrs Fisher's late husband was a German! And that her name is really spelt, F-I-S-C-H-E-R!"

"Cor!" Elvira gasped, wide-eyed, "So that's why she was on the Germans' side!"

"No! No! It wasn't that!" Mrs Honeyball was almost tripping over her tongue in her eagerness to tell her tale. "The beginning of it all was that she was plain scared silly in case anyone found out about her husband. That was why she came here from London, so P.C. Appleby says."

"But why was she a spy, then?" Elvira asked, screwing her face up with the effort of trying to follow Mrs Honeyball's train of thought.

"Ah, well! That was her craftiness, wasn't it?" Mrs Honeyball replied enigmatically. "You see, it turns out the late Mr Fischer had lots of relatives in Germany. Brothers, nephews and cousins. That sort of thing. And of course at the start of the War they're called up for the army! And when they open the prisoner-of-war camp down at the Old Factory, Mother Fischer starts worrying herself sick in case any of her German in-laws are sent here and they recognize her and give her secret away!"

Elvira frowned. "Yes," she said slowly. "So that explains why she kept on about having the Camp moved away. But I still don't understand about the spy bit, Mrs Honeyball."

"It was desperation, my love!" Mrs Honeyball's round face was quite flushed with excitement as she continued. "It was the only thing Mrs Fischer could think of to have the Camp moved. She thought if she could frighten us into believing that a spy was in the district who must be in league with the prisoners, then we'd all get so worked up that they'd have to move the Camp. So she left those field-glasses where she knew that Sophie would find them . . ."

But Elvira's mind was running on ahead. "What about the Zep?" she asked impatiently. "How did she know that was coming?"

"But she didn't! That was the funniest thing of all!" Mrs Honeyball exclaimed. "According to P.C. Appleby, she'd gone out that night with her old torch hoping someone would see her and it would stir up some more trouble. But blow me! If she didn't look up and see that old Zep wandering about up there in the sky! So up she rushes to Mitchells' windmill thinking it's her lucky night. What she wanted, she says, was for the Zep to drop its bombs on the Old Factory and that would really have been the end of the Camp! But she was so worked up and excited she kept signalling the wrong directions to it!"

Thank heavens for that, Elvira thought with a little shiver, as she walked over to put the kettle on and make Mrs Honeyball the cup of tea she was doubtless expecting.

"I suppose we ought to feel sorry for her really," Rhoda remarked that evening, as they sat discussing Mrs Fischer's story after their meal. "She must have been ever so frightened to have acted so wickedly!"

Elvira, who was drawing a railway engine for little Arthur, couldn't feel so charitable and was on the point of saying so when a sudden hammering on the back door interrupted her.

"Whoever can that be knocking the house down!" Rhoda frowned.

But Arthur had already raced into the scullery to pull open the door and reveal Sidney Spurgeon's excited face.

"Please, Mrs Preston, can Elvie come down right now to my dad's barn?" the boy gasped. "Rector sent me up. He says there's something she ought to see."

"Whatever can he mean?" Rhoda asked. Then catching sight of Elvira's expression, she added, "You look as though you know, Elvie. Reckon you'd better be off before you burst with excitement!" For Elvira was already on her feet, her whole face radiant with expectation.

Elvira's boots hammered sparks out of the flints on the Frissington St Peter track as she raced after Sidney. Past the goosegrass path, the Old Rectory, the factory and the shop. Down to the crossroads, then left along the road to Spurgeons' farm. When they reached the barn they were both red-faced and breathless, but they flew straight in through the wide, open door like two homing pigeons.

"Whoah, there! Whoah!" yelled Mr Spurgeon, putting his great, brown hands out to stop their headlong career. But his face was wreathed in smiles. So was that of the rector and of Henry, Mr Spurgeon's labourer. The trio had been gazing down at an object that lay on the barn floor at their feet.

"Come here, Elvira," the Reverend Robson-Turner beamed. "Come and see what Mr Spurgeon and Henry have fished up out of your well this evening."

Elvira dropped on her knees beside the life-size figure of a chubby-limbed boy, arms raised above his head, as though giving a blessing.

163

"It's him, isn't it?" she breathed, lifting her eyes to the rector's. "It's the cherub! Even though he's not golden any more, but all grey and funny like this. I've kept wondering all day. And telling myself not to be stupid — that it couldn't possibly be, that it was only some old statue someone had thrown away."

"Yes. I don't think there's any doubt, my dear," the rector said gently. "If I lift him just a little . . . like this, you can see his folded wings. We've found our golden angel all right," he continued, straightening up. "Mr Spurgeon and Henry discovered the ledge built into the side of the well where he'd been lying in all his tarpaulin wrappings. The bomb-blast must have dislodged him and he fell into the sludge at the bottom. That's why he's such a dirty cherub at the moment."

"Why don't you bathe him, sir?" Sidney, standing behind Elvira, piped up.

"I wouldn't dare, my lad!" the rector exclaimed in a hushed voice. "Not a treasure like this! He'll have to go up to London to be attended to by experts."

"But he will come back?" Elvira asked anxiously.

"Of course! Of course he will!" the Reverend Robson-Turner assured her. "He'll come back to take his place in his own church in his own village. And who knows? Perhaps by Christmas this frightful war will be over and I'll be holding services in Frissington Angel again."

"Oh, I must go now!" Elvira exclaimed abruptly, as she jumped to her feet. "I'm just bursting to tell my mam! She'll be ever so thrilled to hear the golden angel's back!"

As Elvira raced off with an exuberant farewell wave, Mr Spurgeon took off his old straw hat and scratched his head.

"Funny!" he remarked. "Can't say as I've ever heard Elvira Preston call Rhoda 'Mam' before!"

"Nor me!" Sidney chimed in.

"No, that struck me, too," the Reverend Robson-Turner said with a quiet smile of satisfaction. "It seems our golden angel may have started dispensing his blessings already!"

30

Homecomings

There was to be a golden harvest of happiness for Elvira at the end of that summer.

With the cutting of the oats came the news (brought to her hotfoot one Wednesday morning by the rector) that Bill was to be repatriated to Germany on compassionate grounds so that he could look for his sister.

"If you come down at two o'clock sharp to the Old Factory gates we can wave 'good-bye' to him," the Reverend Robson-Turner had told her. And Elvira had done so, although it had been hard for her to return Bill's delighted smile and hold back the tears that were stabbing behind her eyes, as the army motor disappeared down the hill in a cloud of yellow dust.

When reaping was in full swing in the wheat fields news arrived, not of a departure, but of a homecoming. And so incredible did it seem to Elvira when Rhoda told her that she stood gaping 'like a codfish'.

"The Kindnesses adopting Clarry!" she exclaimed finally when she found her tongue. "But, Mam! That's just . . ."

". . . too wonderful to be true?" Rhoda had chuckled. "But it is true, Elvie! Everything's been arranged and Clarry's coming through to Ipswich next weekend. That's if Miss Kindness doesn't burst with impatience beforehand and rush down to Surrey to kidnap him!"

"And will I be able to visit him?" Elvira asked, her eyes glowing at the realization of her friend's good fortune.

"Any time you want," Rhoda told her. "And Miss Kindness will bring Clarry here of course to visit us."

But it was during the barley harvest that the supreme golden bounty came dropping out of the September sky. Old George, the postman, came panting and wheezing up the Frissington Angel track one Saturday morning on his rattly old bicycle at the unusually early hour of seven-fifteen. Rhoda answered his frantic hammering on the back door, took the pale-blue envelope he handed her and subsequently let out such a screech that Elvira, who had just returned from the well, spilled a whole bucket of water over five indignant red hens which had been pecking about her feet! But it was Elvira who had to attend to the reading of the letter since Rhoda's tears were soon flowing so furiously that she couldn't see. On the back of the envelope beneath some printed foreign words her dad had written his address:

Pte. T. Preston,
4th Battalion Anglian Regiment,
British Prisoner of War,
E.K.I. No. 2 Company,
Jacobsfeld, Germany

"What does he say then, gel? What does he say?" prompted old George impatiently, looking as though he might snatch the letter back at any moment.

With quivering fingers Elvira unfolded the single, lined sheet of paper and began to read.

"My dears," her dad had written on the twenty-third of August, "I hope you hadn't given up hope of me. I was taken in May with thirty others and put in with some French cavalry. We were brought to Germany and have been moved six times since being here. This is why I couldn't get a letter through to you. That, and being with the French instead of with our own lads. Still, I've not been treated badly and our work is with the horses which is up my street. Food's very scarce here so there's talk we might be exchanged for German prisoners very soon and sent home. An old German lady came up to the stables one day and gave me a parcel of underclothes, slippers and boots. They had been her son's. I was very touched. How are my Elvie and my Artie? God willing, I'll be with you all by Christmas. Your loving husband and father, Tom."

"Oh, Elvie! Elvie! I knew it!" Rhoda wailed, embracing Elvira joyfully. "I never gave up hope!"

"Nor me, Mam! Nor me!" Elvira sobbed.

"Same here!" sniffed old George, blowing his nose. "I knew Tom Preston would come bouncing back! Good old Tom!"

"And good old George for bringing us the news!" Rhoda cried, flinging her arms around the old postman's neck.

"Yes! Good old George!" Elvira spluttered, half crying, half laughing. And grabbing his hand and Rhoda's arm she started to haul them round the scullery in a wild, triumphant dance.

Little Artie, who had come slithering downstairs to discover the cause of the commotion, stood in his nightgown in the living-room doorway, his eyes wide with astonishment.

"This is . . . pre-posh-ter-ous!" he brought out eventually. And because it was the longest word he had ever used and he rather liked the sound of it, he said it again, shaking his head and putting his hands on his hips, "Pre-POSH-ter-ous!"

POSTSCRIPT

The dark yew trees outside in the churchyard wore gauzy dresses of white frost. Inside the church all was colour, warmth and radiance. As Miss Allison, with the rector's engagement ring winking like a star on her finger, played the introduction to *The Holly and the Ivy*, Elvira thought there could never be another Christmas morning as perfect as this one. She glanced along the pew to where her dad stood, chin up and eyes shining, holding Arthur's hand. After the church service Dad and Mam would go down to the chapel while Elvira took Artie home and kept her eye on the turkey and the plum-puddings. The Robertsons were coming back to dinner and everything had to be perfect. Then in the afternoon Miss Kindness was calling to take them all over to Ipswich for Christmas tea. Elvira had been invited to stay there for a week and there were plans for her and Clarry to go to the cinema and the theatre, and perhaps have a day up in London.

"O-of all the trees that are in the wood," the choir sang lustily above the organ's voice. Elvira's hand felt for the golden locket that had hung round her neck since yesterday and which held the photograph of a curly-haired girl with laughing eyes.

"This is a Christmas gift to you from Siggi," Bill had written in his letter. "She has started to learn English so that she can one day write to you herself."

How odd that things should have turned out this way, Elvira thought, exchanging a dreamy smile with her mam. Such a wonderful Christmas after that nightmarish summer! The summer she would never forget. The summer of the Zeppelin! Then her gaze moved across to the small side-chapel where the Christmas crib was set up, and where the golden angel, poised gracefully on the wrought-iron stand which Mr Diaper had made, held two lighted candles high above his head. The flames burned steady and bright: two tiny beacons holding a promise of hope for all the summers and winters to come.

"Welcome home, golden angel!" breathed Elvira, as the last notes of the carol faded and the congregation seated themselves again. "Welcome home!"

Heard about the Puffin Club?

. . . it's a way of finding out more about Puffin books and authors, of winning prizes (in competitions), sharing jokes, a secret code, and perhaps seeing your name in print! When you join you get a copy of our magazine, *Puffin Post*, sent to you four times a year, a badge and a membership book.

For details of subscription and an application form, send a stamped addressed envelope to:

The Puffin Club Dept A
Penguin Books Limited
Bath Road
Harmondsworth
Middlesex UB7 ODA

and if you live in Australia, please write to:

The Australian Puffin Club
Penguin Books Australia Limited
P.O. Box 257
Ringwood
Victoria 3134

THE SWORDBEARER